SECRETS OF
BEARHAVEN

BOOK FOUR

BATTLE FOR BEARHAVEN

Don't miss all the exciting adventures!

Secrets of Bearhaven Book 1

Secrets of Bearhaven Book 2:
Mission to Moon Farm

Secrets of Bearhaven Book 3:
Hidden Rock Rescue

SECRETS OF BEARHAVEN

BOOK FOUR

BATTLE FOR BEARHAVEN

K. E. ROCHA

SCHOLASTIC PRESS / NEW YORK

Library of Congress Cataloging-in-Publication Data

Names: Rocha, K. E., author.
Title: Battle for Bearhaven / K. E. Rocha.
Description: First edition. | New York, NY : Scholastic Press, 2017. | Series: Secrets of Bearhaven ; Book Four | Summary: Aware that the evil smuggler, Pam, is closing in on their location, the bears of Bearhaven are moving to a new location—but the attack comes too soon, and Spencer Plain and his bear friends, Aldo and Kate, are cut off from Spencer's parents and the other bears, and in serious need of a plan to rescue both themselves and the captive bears that are controlled by Pam.
Identifiers: LCCN 2017017546 (print) | LCCN 2017020588 (ebook) | ISBN 9780545813198 | ISBN 9780545813068 (hardcover)
Subjects: LCSH: Bears—Juvenile fiction. | Human-animal Communication—Juvenile fiction. | Rescues—Juvenile fiction. | Friendship—Juvenile fiction. | CYAC: Bears—Fiction. | Human-animal communication—Fiction. | Rescues—Fiction. | Friendship—Fiction.
Classification: LCC PZ7.1.R637 (ebook) | LCC PZ7.1.R637 Bat 2017 (print) | DDC [Fic]—dc23
LC record available at https://lccn.loc.gov/2017017546

10 9 8 7 6 5 4 3 2 1   17 18 19 20 21

Printed in the U.S.A.   23

First edition, September 2017
Book design by Nina Goffi

For my family, and the anbrandas *who have become my family. And for Sonny, my next chapter, with love.*

SECRETS OF BEARHAVEN

BOOK FOUR

BATTLE FOR BEARHAVEN

1

"RED ALERT! RED ALERT!" A shout tore through the woods around Spencer Plain. He jumped to his feet. Kate Weaver, the bear cub beside him, scrambled to all fours.

"We can't leave the rope!" she exclaimed, her eyes wide as she looked down to the forest floor, to the knot game Spencer had set up for them to play. It could give them away if anyone noticed it.

"I'll move it—you go hide!" Spencer tried not to sound frantic, but it seemed like the trees had come to life all around them. The wide trunks quaked, and the branches and leaves shook as Bearhaven bears responded to the red alert, climbing as fast and as high as they could. The bears were hiding. A red alert meant that Pam, the bear smuggler with an army of eighty-eight microchipped bears, who wanted to destroy Bearhaven, had arrived in the forest.

But how?! Spencer thought. It was too soon!

"Red alert!" the warning call came again but from farther away. The other groups of bears were picking up the alarm and passing it along through the woods.

"Kate, hurry!" Spencer urged his best friend. "I'll be right behind you! Just hide!" He reached forward and switched off Kate's BEAR-COM, the translating device around her neck. The first thing the bears were supposed to do in a red alert was turn off their BEAR-COMs, but Kate seemed frozen. Spencer didn't blame her. Kate had been captured once before by Pam's evil lackeys. She knew exactly how cruel Pam could be, and she had the scar on her ear to remind her.

"Galuk!" Spencer begged her to hurry in Ragayo, the bears' language. Now that her BEAR-COM was switched off, speaking in Ragayo was the only way Kate would understand him. Finally, she started to move. She swung her chestnut-colored head back and forth, scanning the trees and sniffing hard, then turned and ran into the woods.

Spencer dropped back to his knees, grabbing for the rope. He cast an anxious glance over his shoulder but didn't see anyone coming . . . yet. As quickly as he could, he started to untie the game of knots that ran between two raised tree roots. As he worked, he tried to make sense of what had gone wrong. Pam and his bear army were not supposed to be here for another week! And by then, Bearhaven's bears had planned to be far away, safe from Pam's attack.

How could Evarita have been so wrong? he wondered. Evarita, a Bearhaven operative, was supposed to be spying on Pam and updating the Bear Council on Pam's movements. Just this morning, she'd said he was still at his illegal bear smuggling facility, Moon Farm!

Crunch! Crunch! Crunch!

Spencer froze at the sound of heavy footsteps. *Lots* of heavy footsteps. The trees around him were completely still. Bearhaven's bears must all be well hidden by now.

2

"Galuk!" a bear called down from a nearby tree.

Spencer looked down at his rope—three more knots to go! His fingers flew, tugging and pulling every which way until it was free.

Crunch! Crunch! The footsteps were getting louder. Spencer sprang to his feet and broke into a sprint, the length of rope bundled in one hand. He ran in the direction Kate had, away from the threatening footsteps.

"Kate!" he whispered once as he ran, hoping to join her in whatever hiding spot she'd found. But there was no answer. She must not have heard him. Spencer searched the trees, but the bears were so well hidden he didn't see any of them. Then Aldo Weaver, Kate's oldest brother, suddenly lurched down through thick leafy branches. The bear silently jerked his head toward the foliage above, then returned to cover, disappearing the way he'd come.

A low rumble startled Spencer just as he reached the tree Aldo was hiding in. He spun around, his backpack pressed against the tree trunk.

Crunch! Crunch! Crunch!

The heavy footsteps were heading straight for him from the right, but the rumbling sound was coming from the left, and it was getting louder. Spencer squinted into the trees, afraid to find out what it was, but determined to know.

"Hruk!" Aldo growled down, urging Spencer to come, but Spencer didn't budge. He could just make out the shadow of a large vehicle moving through the woods.

"Ko!" Aldo grunted the bears' word for "now," then leaned out of the tree, his jaws open wide, and clamped the back of Spencer's T-shirt between his teeth. The bear gave a

strong yank, pulling Spencer off his feet, and deposited him roughly onto a low branch. Not a second later, headlights rolled over the tree trunk below, lighting the place where Spencer had just been. But Spencer hardly noticed. His eyes were locked on the source of the headlights—a black Hummer rumbling through the woods, its windows tinted. Behind the Hummer, a row of pickup trucks bumped down the dirt path in a long, ominous line.

CRUNCH! CRUNCH! CRUNCH!

Over the thundering sound of footsteps, Spencer could just barely hear Aldo retreating to a hiding spot higher up in the tree. He moved to follow but realized he was too late.

Four bears were emerging from the trees to Spencer's right, and behind them were four more bears. Row after

row of bears appeared, each one no more than a step away from the row in front of it. Each bear moved in perfect step with all the others, their paws landing heavily, almost mechanically, as they marched. After six rows of bears had marched through the trees, a row of four human guards followed. Each one was toting an enormous tranquilizer gun. At the sight of the tranquilizers, Spencer scrambled back in horror, pressing himself against the wide tree trunk. *They're really here,* he thought. *And they mean business.*

2

Spencer stared, wide eyed, down at the bear army marching beneath the branch he was crouched on. There were six rows of guards, and twenty-two rows of bears—Spencer counted them as they passed.

"They're being controlled right now," Spencer whispered to himself, relaxing a little. He'd been this close to Pam's bear army before. Each member of the bear army was implanted with a microchip that allowed Pam or one of his employees to control the bear with a remote. The microchipped bears were terrifying, but when they were being controlled by remote, they couldn't act on any of their own instincts, only follow orders. They wouldn't be able to so much as turn their heads even if they smelled Spencer or any of Bearhaven's bears now.

Spencer grasped the branch he was on and strained his ears, listening. The last rows of bears had disappeared into the woods in the direction of Bearhaven. "I think the coast is clear," Spencer whispered once the woods were quiet again.

"It smells that way," Aldo answered as he climbed through the thick branches toward Spencer. The green ON light on his BEAR-COM glowed. "But what are they doing here?" The big black-and-brown bear crouched on a branch nearby.

"I have no idea," Spencer said quietly. "Evarita was definitely wrong about Pam's location, that's for sure."

"She said he and his army wouldn't be arriving here for another week, right?" Aldo sounded just as confused as Spencer felt.

"At least everyone's already out of Bearhaven," Spencer answered. To prepare for Pam's attack, all of Bearhaven's bears had been broken up into sleuths—groups of five bears who would stick together—and evacuated into the surrounding woods a few days ago to hide out until it was their turn to be relocated to a safer place by Spencer's parents. Mom, Dad, and Uncle Mark had a plan to move the bears to a new plot of land a day's drive north of here, but they couldn't move all the bears at once without risking Pam finding out about it. "My parents and Uncle Mark aren't even here," he remembered, thinking out loud. "Mom and Dad left a few hours ago to take the first thirty bears to the new Bearhaven. And Uncle Mark is already up there, installing the security."

"I know," Aldo said solemnly. "Let's go. We have to get to the checkpoint, and I want to make sure Kate's not too scared."

"Good idea," Spencer answered right away. "She was definitely shaken up by the red alert." He was, too, and now that he'd seen Pam's army up close, he didn't think that feeling would go away any time soon.

Aldo took one more big whiff of air, then, having confirmed that the coast really was clear, jumped from the tree to the ground. Spencer shoved his tangled-up length of rope into his backpack, stalling a bit, then carefully climbed down after Aldo. By the time he'd reached the forest floor, Aldo had already set off at a run and was reaching the tree that served as their sleuth's checkpoint.

Spencer broke into a jog to catch up, even though he didn't need Aldo's help to find the checkpoint. Everyone in the sleuth Spencer, Aldo, and Kate were assigned to reported back there each evening. By now, Spencer was sure he'd be able to find this tree from anywhere in the woods, and he knew the bears could find it easily using their sense of smell.

Spencer pulled himself up into the tree and immediately found himself face-to-face with Bearhaven's biggest black bear, B.D., the Head of the Bear Guard, Bearhaven's security, as well as the head of sleuth number one.

"Have you seen Kate?" B.D. asked.

"No, not since she went to hide," Spencer answered, bewildered. "I thought she'd be here." He looked around, but Kate definitely wasn't in the tree. There were B.D., his brother John Shirley, and their four-month-old nephew, Darwin, the prized cub who Spencer had only just helped to rescue from Pam two weeks ago.

"I need to check in with the other sleuths," B.D. said gruffly, as though frustrated that Kate was taking so long to join them. "Everyone stay here. I'll have a plan for how to deal with Pam's unexpected early arrival when I get back."

Once B.D. had left to make sure that the rest of Bearhaven's bears had made it to their checkpoints, Aldo spoke up. "John Shirley, when he gets back, please tell B.D.

that Spencer and I went to get Kate," he said. Spencer looked up at the bear, startled. Aldo Weaver never disobeyed orders from B.D.! Well . . . that wasn't exactly true. Spencer had seen Aldo do something he wasn't supposed to once before, but that was only because Kate was in grave danger.

Is Aldo that worried?

"You sure you want to do that?" John Shirley asked.

"We'll be back as soon as we have her," Aldo replied, avoiding the question. He shot Spencer a look, then climbed out of the tree as fast as he could. Spencer hurried to follow.

"What's going on?!" he whispered as soon as they were both on the ground.

"Climb on." Aldo dodged yet another question and instead crouched low. Spencer hesitated but not for long. He and Aldo had been on two high-stakes missions together. They were teammates, and by the bears' definition of the word, they were also family. Spencer knew he could trust the bear. He grabbed two fistfuls of Aldo's fur and swung onto Aldo's back. Aldo immediately launched into a run, heading in the very same direction Pam's army was marching.

"Aldo, where are we going?" Spencer asked, his stomach twisting. He was afraid he already knew the answer.

"Bearhaven," Aldo said grimly. "I can smell Kate. She went back there."

3

Spencer held tight to Aldo as the bear ran at top speed through the woods toward Bearhaven. Spencer's mind was racing. There was nowhere more dangerous for Kate, or any bear, to be than Bearhaven right now. Pam's army of microchipped bears and guards were probably closing in on Bearhaven's outer wall this very minute, preparing for their attack. And if Kate was the only bear inside Bearhaven when Pam's army got there, she'd be their only target!

Spencer gripped Aldo's fur even harder, his stomach twisting anxiously as he imagined Kate facing Pam and the entire bear army alone. He wished they could go faster, but he could feel Aldo panting beneath him. They were already moving as fast as they could.

"We'll go in across the bridge in the treetops," Aldo called up to Spencer, quickly outlining a plan. "But we're going to have to avoid being seen by Pam's army."

"Definitely," Spencer called back, trying to sound confident. The Bear Council had declared Bearhaven strictly off-limits now that the evacuation had started. It was too dangerous to go back. But off-limits or not, if Kate

10

was inside, Spencer and Aldo had to go in. They couldn't leave Kate in there alone.

"Then we find Kate," Aldo went on. "We'll get her and get out as quickly as we can." Aldo's voice dropped a little bit lower. "We shouldn't risk talking again until we're clear of Pam's army. And, sorry, little man, I'm afraid there are going to be a lot of ups and downs on our way."

"Okay." Spencer tightened his grip on Aldo's fur. He hated heights. Specifically, Spencer hated the idea of falling from high heights, and Aldo knew that. But the fastest way for them to get into Bearhaven and to reach Kate was by going up. Way up.

Spencer scanned the ground as Aldo raced across it. It was covered in bear tracks.

Kirby is going to have a field day when she sees these, he thought. Spencer knew it wouldn't be long before Kirby saw the tracks. She lived alone with her mom, who worked a lot, and when her mom was away, Kirby studied the woods. She was so determined to uncover the reason for the suspicious bear activity that she had homemade surveillance set up in the trees. Until now, the Bear Guard had been able to avoid Kirby's surveillance systems and keep almost all the important information about Bearhaven a secret from her, but Spencer didn't think there was much anyone could do about the trail of bear tracks leading straight to Bearhaven now.

Bearhaven wasn't the only thing the tracks led to, though. Wherever they stopped, eighty-eight microchipped bears were waiting. Aldo must have gotten the same idea, because a second later, he took a sharp left and wove at a dangerously high speed through an even more dense area of the woods until he reached a break in the trees, where finally, he skidded to a stop.

Straight ahead, across a dirt path, were the tightly packed trees and gnarled roots that made up Bearhaven's outer wall. Aldo sniffed the air. Somewhere down this path, at another section of Bearhaven's wall, Pam and his two evil employees, Margo and Ivan Lalicki, were probably trying to break into what they thought was a valley filled with bears. Spencer hoped it would take them a very long time to get through. He and Aldo needed as much time as possible to find Kate and get her out of there.

Spencer felt Aldo's muscles tense. Then the bear lunged forward, crossed the path in two strides, and launched himself at a tree. He started to scale the tree's massive trunk. Spencer held tight to Aldo's back, his heart hammering in his chest. The ground was getting farther and farther below them, but out of the corner of his eye, Spencer spotted movement there. He glanced down.

"Oh no," he whispered, immediately regretting looking down. His mind quickly filled with images of himself plummeting the distance down to the forest's floor, just like it always did when Spencer was high off the ground. And to make matters worse, now that Spencer had seen the ground below, he knew, if they survived the climb, what they'd be facing if they didn't make it back out of Bearhaven before Pam made it in.

Pam's army was still organized in rows. And all together, the group of eighty-eight bears looked enormous, flanked by guards and surrounded by a fleet of trucks—for transporting the bears Pam planned to capture, Spencer guessed. He thought back to his first run-in with a microchipped bear. It had been on his first-ever bear rescue mission. Margo, Pam's horrible employee, had turned a bear on him just to prove how powerful the microchip technology really was. She'd used the remote to command the bear to attack, and if there hadn't been a wall between Spencer and that bear, Spencer was sure the bear would have killed him. In fact, under Margo's control, the microchipped bear had been so vicious, Spencer had been afraid it would find a way to crash straight through the wall.

"Hold on," Aldo muttered. Before Spencer could answer, his fear of the microchipped bears was again replaced by his original, more immediate fear: his terror of falling. They were airborne, midleap from the treetop to the hidden bridge that spanned Bearhaven's outer wall.

Aldo landed steadily. It looked like they were standing in between two leafy treetops, suspended in the air by . . . nothing. But Spencer knew better than to panic. He'd made this crossing enough times to know the bridge was there. Even though he couldn't *see* the bridge, it was there, hidden by a hologram that matched the rest of the treetops so that it could never be spotted from above.

"Down we go," Aldo said, moving quickly. Before Spencer's fear of falling could take over, Aldo's four paws were hitting the ground inside Bearhaven with a single soft thud.

"We're in," Spencer said, relieved.

"What's that?" Aldo answered, slowly turning around to face the wall of trees they'd just crossed over.

"I said—" Spencer started, but Aldo cut him off.

"No, I mean, what's that sound?"

Spencer strained his ears, trying to make out whatever it was Aldo had heard.

"Chain saws . . ." he whispered. "Lots of them."

"What?" the bear asked.

Spencer gulped. The metallic growls of the saws were getting louder, filling the air. "They're going to cut through the wall."

4

Spencer and Aldo were just reaching the top of the hill overlooking Bearhaven's valley when the first tree fell. The terrible sound of chain saws chomping through wood had followed them all the way as they ran from the clearing inside the wall to the hilltop, but it wasn't until they paused to scan the abandoned Bearhaven for Kate that they heard the first tree actually go down.

Spencer flinched, listening to the tree crack against the ones around it on its way to the ground. He felt Aldo tense, but the bear didn't take his eyes off Bearhaven.

Spencer had never seen the valley look so still. He tightened his grip on Aldo's fur. Bearhaven looked like a ghost town. The stillness felt ominous. The paths that wove in and out of the bears' dome-shaped homes were empty. The flags that usually flew in Bearhaven's center had been taken down during the evacuation. There wasn't even a glint of sunlight on the metal over the Lab, because the Lab had been hidden from view by holograms to stop Pam from discovering the incredible high-tech work that Bearhaven's bears did there.

Another tree crashed down, making Spencer flinch

again, and this time, the loud bang it made had the effect on Aldo of a gunshot at the start of a race. Aldo sprinted down the hill, careening into the town. They were going so fast that Spencer had to duck his head low, pressing his face into the back of Aldo's neck to stop his eyes from watering. He didn't have to look up to know that they were heading straight for the Weavers' house. Aldo's family's house had been Spencer's home, too, ever since he'd found out about Bearhaven, and he knew the path by heart.

"We're here," Aldo practically yelled only moments later, skidding to a stop so roughly that Spencer was almost tossed off the bear's back. Spencer jumped to the ground, and a moment later, Aldo was striding up to the front door. He headbutted it open and went in, bellowing, "Kate!"

"Kate?" Spencer joined in, rushing inside. He pushed the door shut behind him to block out the awful buzz of chain saws, then followed Aldo down the stairs toward Kate's bedroom. But when the bear reached the door, he stopped and spun around, approaching Spencer's bedroom instead.

"In here," he said, pushing the door open. Spencer ran in after him and flicked on the lights.

"Kate!" he exclaimed. Spencer could just see one of her back paws poking out from under the bottom bunk of his bed.

At the sound of their voices, Kate scrambled on her belly halfway out from underneath the bed, grumbling Ragayo Spencer couldn't understand. *Her BEAR-COM is still off,* he realized, and crouched down beside Kate to turn the device back on for her.

"No, they're not gone," Aldo answered his sister. "But, Kate, we have to get out of here!"

Kate scooted back under the bunk bed again. "Not until they're gone!" she called. Aldo and Spencer exchanged a look.

"Kate, you know Bearhaven is off-limits," Aldo pressed. "You weren't supposed to come back. It's way more dangerous to be in here right now than it is to be in the woods."

"I didn't know where else to go," Kate answered softly. Spencer wasn't surprised. Kate had lived in Bearhaven her entire life, and the only time she'd been outside Bearhaven's wall she'd been kidnapped. The woods were probably almost as scary to her as the threat of the bear army.

"Kate," Spencer jumped in, thinking back to his first night in Bearhaven. "Do you remember the first time you slept under my bunk bed?"

"Yes."

"You said it was because you didn't want me to be afraid without my parents, and you thought I'd feel better if you were here," Spencer went on, relieved when Kate poked her head out from under the bunk. "Well, I *did* feel better. And now we need to stick together so that we can all be brave and get out of here before—"

"Before what?"

Spencer immediately swallowed his words. He looked at Aldo.

"Before Pam's army gets in," Aldo said flatly.

Kate's eyes widened, but she didn't hide. "Are they close?" she whispered. "To getting in?"

"Yes," Aldo answered. "Very close."

All of a sudden, Kate scrambled out from under the bed. "Well, what are we waiting for?!" she cried. "We. Have. To. GO!"

Spencer leaped to his feet as Kate barreled past him, heading for the hallway. Aldo and Spencer followed her, catching up as she raced up the stairs, through the living room, and out the front door. But the second Spencer burst out of the Weavers' house and onto their sun-soaked front path, he knew there was a problem. The valley was quiet. Too quiet.

"Aldo!" he called. "Kate!" The bears were already rushing down the main path, heading in the direction of the hilltop Spencer and Aldo had just come from. Both bears stopped running, turning back with puzzled looks on their faces. They crossed the distance back to him in a few paces, but Spencer wasn't looking at Aldo and Kate anymore.

"What's wrong?" Aldo asked.

Spencer didn't answer. Instead, he lifted a shaky hand and pointed to the hilltop that overlooked all of Bearhaven. A black Hummer sat at the top of the hill. Two pickup trucks appeared on either side of it. Aldo and Kate spun around just as the rows of bears began to fan out along the ridge.

Aldo was the only one who seemed able to speak. "They're here."

5

"Don't move," Spencer said quietly, his eyes locked on the bear army that loomed on the hilltop. He wasn't sure he, Kate, or Aldo, would be *able* to move yet, even if they wanted to. They were frozen in place on the Weavers' front path, afraid to attract attention and not sure what to do next.

"What are we going to do?" Kate whispered.

"We can hide in the house," Spencer said, thinking aloud. "We could barricade the door. They'd have to give up eventually." As soon as he said it, Spencer knew his plan probably wouldn't work.

"There are eighty-eight of them, plus the guards," Aldo answered, echoing Spencer's thoughts. "I don't think we'd be able to keep them out. Not without sealing the doors and windows in lockdown mode. And the only way to activate lockdown is from the Lab."

If only there was someone in the Lab who could—wait a minute . . . Spencer thought. "The Lab!" he exclaimed, a little more loudly than he should have. His eyes flew back up to the hilltop, and to his relief, everyone up there seemed to be distracted by something. For a second, Spencer was distracted by it, too.

Pam had emerged from inside the Hummer and was standing on the vehicle's hood. Spencer could only just barely make out the evil man. Pam's black hair, which was always perfectly gelled into a sleek wave above his forehead, gleamed in the sunlight. By the way Pam was making big dramatic gestures toward his audience, which included, Spencer assumed, his guards and Margo and Ivan, it looked like Pam was making some grand speech. If there was anything Pam loved more than power, or himself, it was attention.

Disgusted but eager to take advantage of the time Pam's theatrics had bought them, Spencer looked back to Kate and Aldo.

"We have to get to the Lab," he said.

"I was thinking the same thing," Aldo replied right away.

"So let's go!" Kate chimed in.

"The hard part is getting there safely." Aldo's voice was low, like he was concentrating on the path through Bearhaven they'd have to take to the Lab. Spencer started to think it through himself. The Lab was on the opposite side of Bearhaven from where they stood. There was no way they'd be able to get all the way there unseen, and once Pam's army spotted them . . . He pushed the thought out of his mind. The Lab was the only place they'd be safe. They *had* to find a way to get there.

Spencer looked to the row of houses on the opposite side of the path. "I think we can get as far as Raymond's without anyone spotting us," he said, "if we cross to the other side of this path while Pam's still making his big speech, then stay close to the houses the whole way."

"Let's get over there now, while Pam is demanding they pay attention to him," Aldo said. "But slowly. No sudden movements."

"And together," Spencer added. He stepped in between the two bears so that he, Kate, and Aldo were side by side and could move as a single unit. He glanced back up at the hill. Pam was still parading around on the hood of the Hummer. "Let's go." He took a slow step forward. Kate and Aldo stayed glued to his sides. They got the hang of it after one more step and moved forward like a single slow-motion blob wading through a pool of honey. They reached the opposite side of the path within a minute. Once they were there, they each flattened themselves against the closest house. Spencer strained his ears, afraid they had been spotted and he'd hear shouts and orders to attack, but he didn't hear anything. "Did they see us?" he whispered to Aldo and Kate, not sure he could trust his human ears.

"It doesn't sound that way," Aldo said. "Let's get moving." With that, the bear turned and started to run in the direction of Bearhaven's one restaurant, Raymond's Café. Aldo stayed so close to the houses that his fur brushed against them with every step. Kate followed, copying her brother, and Spencer brought up the rear at a sprint. The restaurant was across another open pathway, but Spencer knew the larger buildings that lined the field at Bearhaven's center would hide them from view of Pam and his army.

Aldo lunged across the path and into Raymond's with

Kate and Spencer sticking close behind. Spencer swung the door shut, then ran to a window at the far edge of the restaurant. Through it he could just see a small section of the hilltop, and the army poised for attack there.

"They haven't moved!" he called to Aldo and Kate. Aldo was pacing back and forth, just inside the closed front door, and Kate was panting, but she didn't seem as afraid as she had before.

"We made it!" she practically cheered.

"So far," Aldo answered grimly. Kate's ears drooped. "I only mean we should get ready for the next stretch," Aldo added more cheerfully, trying to keep Kate's spirits up.

Spencer scanned the restaurant, wondering what they could do to prepare for the next, way more dangerous stretch. He went to the back of the restaurant, to Raymond's kitchen, and started to look around for something he could use to fight off Pam's army while Aldo outlined the plan for the next leg of their run to the Lab.

"We're going to have to make a break for it," Aldo said. "As soon as we're ready. We'll go out the back door and head straight for the Bear Guard training field. By the time we leave this building, we'll be out in plain sight, so we're just going to have to outrun them. Spencer will be on my back, and, Kate, you stay beside me. Just run as fast as you can."

Spencer nodded, agreeing with the plan even though he had one big worry. They might be able to outrun the bears . . . but how far could the guards shoot tranquilizer darts? He was just looking over a stack of bear-sized metal baking sheets when Kate trotted into the kitchen.

"Now is not the time to look for snacks!" she exclaimed.

"I wasn't . . ." Spencer started. He looked back and forth between Kate and the baking sheets. "Aldo!" he cried, excited. An idea was starting to take shape in his mind. Spencer slipped his backpack off his back and let it fall to the ground. Then he grabbed for two of the baking sheets. A second later, Aldo joined them in the kitchen.

"Pam and his army are still on the hill, but I don't think we should wait much longer," Aldo said, then seemed to realize that Spencer was pulling ropes out of his backpack. "What's going on?" the bear asked.

"I have an idea," Spencer started to explain, his hands already moving across the rope, quickly wrapping and knotting it across one of the oversized baking sheets. "To protect you two from getting hit with tranquilizer darts." Spencer left a small length of rope free, then picked up the second baking sheet and wrapped and knotted another section of the rope around it.

"Tranquilizer darts?!" Kate shrank back a few steps.

"It's okay, Kate," Spencer went on excitedly. "You're going to have armor!"

Aldo and Kate exchanged a look, but Spencer just kept working.

"Kate, will you come stand here?" he said, pointing to a spot right in front of himself. Kate padded forward, tentatively, until she was standing on all fours in front of Spencer. He slung the rope over her back so that a big baking sheet hung down on either side of her, covering both sides of her body with metal. By now, each of the baking sheets was held tightly in place by two firm lark's head knots and a sheepshank knot. They weren't going anywhere. Spencer crouched down and secured the free ends of the rope under Kate's belly with a few more knots, binding the makeshift armor in place. "Does that feel okay?" he asked, stepping back to examine his work.

Kate wiggled a little. "It feels a little funny," she admitted, "but if it stops the darts from hitting me, I don't mind one bit!"

"Good work, Spencer," Aldo said, looking Kate over. "Can you make me one?"

"Of course," Spencer said, grabbing the two biggest baking sheets in the stack. Each one would have covered his kitchen table at home! "These won't slow you down too much?" he asked, showing Aldo the metal sheets he'd chosen.

"Not more than a tranquilizer dart would," Aldo answered soberly, then stepped in front of Spencer, ready to get his baking-sheet armor.

"What about you?" Aldo asked once he'd been outfitted with a metal shield on either side of his body.

Spencer stood up and put his backpack on.

"I don't think they'll be aiming for me," he said. "But I have my backpack for some protection." He looked back and forth between the newly armored bears. "Ready?"

"Let's go." Kate puffed out her chest to show her bravery.

"Climb on," Aldo said, and crouched low enough that the baking sheets scraped against the ground. Spencer climbed onto Aldo's back, slipping a leg between the bear's body and his armor on either side, and got a firm grip of the fur at Aldo's neck. He looked over Aldo's head to the back door of Raymond's Café. Once they left this building, they wouldn't be safe again until they reached the Lab.

If they made it that far.

6

Spencer clung tightly to Aldo's back, bracing himself as they raced out from behind Raymond's Café.

"Aldo, look!" he cried. Pam's bear army was already on the move, flooding down into the valley. It looked as though they'd been sent in to search Bearhaven. The bears were all running at full speed, breaking out of their rows to spread out in every direction.

"What is it?!" Kate called. Aldo had told his little sister to stay close to him on his right side, so that even if they were overtaken by Pam's bear army, the microchipped bears would have to get through Aldo before they could touch Kate. Aldo was blocking her view of the microchipped bears pouring into Bearhaven now.

"Just keep running!" Aldo answered, picking up his pace.

"FIRST TARGET SPOTTED!" a sudden shriek blared out over Bearhaven. Spencer looked up to the hilltop. The Hummer and pickup trucks were all still poised there. "I see them!" Pam's shouts blasted out of some speaker system Spencer couldn't make out from so far away. He flinched with every word. "Margo, redirect the army! Get them!"

From his position on Aldo's back, Spencer watched in horror as the bear army changed course. They zeroed in on Spencer, Aldo, and Kate and started heading toward them at full speed in a thundering herd.

As three trucks accelerated down the hill and into the valley, Spencer had to resist the urge to yell for Aldo and Kate to run faster—he knew they were already running as fast as they could.

The pickup trucks fell in behind the pack of eighty-eight charging bears, and Spencer could see three guards in the back of each truck, each one brandishing a tranquilizer gun as the trucks sped closer and closer.

"We're almost at the Bear Guard training field!" he called out. They'd be halfway to the Lab at that point. Spencer glanced back over his shoulder. The bear army was gaining on them. The first row of charging bears was already clearing the center of Bearhaven, and showed no signs of slowing down.

"Make them go *faster*, Margo!" Pam's voice demanded.

Please, please, don't go faster, Spencer willed the microchipped bears. But by the way the thundering footsteps suddenly got louder behind him, Spencer knew that Margo had already followed her boss's orders just by pressing a button on her remote. Spencer didn't look back. He, Aldo, and Kate were just reaching the Bear Guard training field. The boulders that the Bear Guard recruits used to build strength were scattered throughout it.

"Kate, stay right behind me!" Aldo shouted as he started to weave his way through the boulders at top speed. When they came out from behind the first boulder and headed for the next, they were met by a huffing, grunting bear. Another one was approaching from the opposite side. Both bears were bigger than Aldo and almost four times Kate's size.

"They're trying to surround us!" Spencer yelled. More bears were peeling away from the pack behind them, trying to get ahead and cut them off.

Aldo didn't answer—he and Kate just dodged behind another boulder and sprinted straight for the next, racing as fast as they could toward the tree line on the opposite side of the field. It seemed like huffing bears were all around them now. Some swatted the ground as they ran; others had started making the horrible jaw-popping sounds that Spencer knew showed a bear's growing aggression.

"Aldo, watch out!" Spencer cried. The three pickup trucks had pulled up next to the bear army and were fast approaching. One pulled up alongside them but didn't attempt to weave through the boulders. Instead, it slowed down, allowing the guards to lift their tranquilizer guns and take steady aim. Spencer pressed himself flat against Aldo's back. Aldo was straining to pick up speed. Kate was running hard beside him, but Spencer was afraid she wouldn't be able to keep it up much longer.

When Spencer, Aldo, and Kate emerged from behind the next boulder, the guards unleashed their first round of shots.

Ping! Ping! Ping! The darts hit the metal sheet on Aldo's side and dropped to the ground.

"Yes!" Spencer shouted. The armor was working!

Ping! Spencer whipped his head around. Another pickup truck had pulled alongside them and was shooting at Kate! The cub stumbled. *No!* If Kate fell now, there'd be no hope of escaping! Luckily, Kate recovered and kept sprinting ahead. None of the darts had hit their mark.

Spencer looked to the line of trees that bordered the far side of the training field. *The trucks won't be able to get through the trees from this direction!* He realized with relief as another shower of darts hit the metal baking sheets strapped to Aldo's and Kate's sides.

Ping! Ping!

The bear army was crowding around Spencer, Aldo, and Kate now, getting closer and closer on either side, but none of the bears had pulled ahead of them enough to block their path to the trees, and none of the bears in the bear army had made the move to attack.

Jaw pops, grunts, and huffs filled the air. One of the larger bears lunged at Kate, a clawed paw outstretched, but Kate dodged behind the last boulder on the field just in time, and the blow from the bear landed on the rock instead.

"We're going to make it!" Spencer yelled over the sound of more darts hitting metal. The trees were only a few paces away now.

"Aim for their heads!" one guard shouted to the others from the closest truck.

"You're too late!" Spencer shouted back, furious, just as Aldo and Kate burst through the narrow gap between two trees and into the woods. The bear army followed them in, and none of the bears slowed their pace, but Spencer turned back to see all three pickup trucks slamming on their brakes. They couldn't get through.

"Follow them! We have to find another way in!" a guard yelled as the ones with tranquilizer guns hopped to the ground and started into the woods on foot. Spencer turned away. *They'll never reach us before we get to the Lab,* he thought.

"Spencer, stay low!" Aldo suddenly shouted. Up ahead, the first bear in Pam's army had cut off the path to the Lab. He was rising up onto his hind legs now, swatting his paws at Aldo as he boomed a low threatening grunt.

"Ah!" Spencer flattened himself against Aldo's back just as Aldo launched himself straight at the bear, headbutting him in the stomach. The bear swatted his front paws only a few inches above Spencer's and Aldo's heads as he stumbled backward. Aldo dodged to one side of the unsteady, furious bear and continued his race to the Lab. Spencer checked that Kate was still right beside them. She was. But she was panting hard now, and she was flanked by enormous, vicious-looking bears.

The clearing came into view, and for a second, Spencer's stomach flipped over, even though he'd known about the hologram. Where the Lab always stood was a row of tall, tightly packed trees that shimmered a little—they weren't real. They were a series of elaborate holograms.

The bear army started to slow, approaching the trees. But Aldo headed straight toward the holograms and, with Kate close by his side, ran directly through. Spencer didn't feel a thing, not that he expected to, when they passed through the hologram, and the Lab suddenly loomed directly in front of them. The shining, dome-shaped building was really there, and the hologram designed to hide it had confused Pam's bears enough to buy Spencer, Aldo, and Kate a few extra seconds. Aldo skidded to a stop in front of the Lab just as the bear army started to get through the hologram and close in on them again.

Aldo leaned toward the metal wall of the Lab and let out a great huff, blasting his breath against the special metal that sealed the Lab shut. Responding to the DNA in Aldo's breath, the metal wall peeled apart to reveal an opening in the side of the Lab.

Aldo spun around and started to back through the opening. He batted his claws at the bears who were only a few feet away now, gathering in a massive crowd of bared teeth.

"Kate, come on!" Spencer yelled at the cub, who was backing toward the Lab, cowering beneath three bears who had risen up onto their hind legs and were glaring down at her. "Kate, now!" Kate turned and ran straight through the opening in the side of the Lab. Once she was through, Aldo shuffled backward into the building, still threatening the bears around them, trying to hold them off long enough for the door in the Lab to shut. Just as it started to, Spencer spotted the first guard stepping past the hologram, his tranquilizer gun raised.

The opening in the side of the Lab snapped shut in the exact same moment that the first of Pam's bears lunged after Spencer, Aldo, and Kate. A muffled thud followed, which Spencer guessed was the sound of the bear unexpectedly slamming into the Lab's smooth outer wall. Then there was a soft *Ping! Ping! Ping!* The guard was shooting. But he was too late.

7

Inside the Lab, Spencer jumped off Aldo's back and immediately crouched down beside the bear to untie the rope binding the makeshift armor to Aldo's body. Both Aldo and Kate were panting hard, and Kate had already dropped to her belly on the sleek white hallway floor, her legs splayed out in four different directions. The baking sheets were spread across her back like metal wings.

The muffled thumps and bangs of the microchipped bears and guards attempting to get into the Lab continued, but Spencer ignored them. He, Aldo, and Kate were safe now. The Lab was made out of a special metal that only opened for bears and humans whose DNA it was programmed to recognize. There wasn't any other way in. At least not that Spencer knew of.

Spencer finished untying the knots around Aldo and pulled the metal sheets away, letting them clatter to the floor.

"That's better," Aldo said, still breathing hard. He shook his whole body, from head to tail. "But there's no question, that armor saved all of us today."

Spencer went to Kate's side.

"Kate?" he said gently. The cub's eyes were closed. "Kate, are you okay?"

"My legs," the cub groaned. "They were not made to go that fast."

"Kate, you were amazing!" Aldo cheered, padding over to his sister's side. "I've never seen a cub run so fast! You're going to make a great Bear Guard recruit one of these days."

Kate opened her eyes and flopped from her belly onto her back so that she could see Aldo and Spencer. The baking sheets scraped against the floor. "If being on the Bear Guard means more of *that*, then no thank you. I'd rather cook like Raymond and eat salmon nuggets all day."

Spencer laughed and reached for the ropes attached to Kate's armor. Once she was free, she rolled back onto her belly and slowly got to all fours. Spencer untied his two ropes from the baking sheets and wound them back up. In the three bear rescue missions he'd been on, and all the training in between, Spencer had learned that rope was the number one thing he always had to have in his mission pack. The rope, and the sailing knots Dad had taught him to tie, had come in handy in plenty of emergencies so far.

"They're not trying to get in anymore," Aldo said, turning back to the sealed silver wall of the Lab. The thumping had stopped, but Spencer wasn't sure if that was a good thing. "Come on, let's see what's going on out there." Aldo set off down the white hallway. He padded along slowly, as though giving himself and Kate a chance to rest their legs.

"I can't believe I'm inside the Lab," Kate whispered to Spencer as they followed Aldo. "All the other cubs are going to be so jealous when they hear about this!"

"Just wait till you see where we're going," Spencer whispered back. The Lab was the most important building in Bearhaven, where lots of top secret business happened, so access to the Lab was restricted to just the bears who needed to be inside. As a member of the Bear Guard, Aldo was allowed in to serve guard duty, but most of Bearhaven's bears didn't even know *how* to get into the building. Spencer wasn't supposed to be in here any more than Kate was, but since arriving in Bearhaven, he'd managed to find himself inside the Lab a few times. Though none of those times had been for very happy occasions.

Just as Spencer had suspected, Aldo turned right into the surveillance room.

"Wow," Kate whispered, her eyes wide.

An enormous bank of screens took up half the room. All of them were on, showing different areas of Bearhaven and its perimeter. Usually, there was a Bear Guard member like Aldo stationed in front of the screens, watching for any suspicious activity. But tonight, the Bear Guard's seat was empty, which gave Spencer a full view of Pam, who was heading straight for the Lab.

Spencer rushed over to the screens for a better look. "Pam's on the move," he said, pointing out the black Hummer as it sped through the valley.

"The bear army is gone!" Kate said a second later, jutting her snout toward the screen that showed the outside of the Lab. She was right. The microchipped bears that had chased Spencer, Aldo, and Kate all the way here had left the area completely. Now four pickup trucks were surrounding the Lab instead. In each truck, guards were ready with tranquilizer guns trained on the building.

"I don't think so," Aldo said. "The bear army is searching the rest of Bearhaven." Spencer scanned the rest of the video feeds from around Bearhaven. Bears seemed to be everywhere *but* the clearing around the Lab now.

"They won't find anyone," Spencer answered, again relieved that Bearhaven's bears had all evacuated a few days ago. "And we're safe in here. There's no way they can get in. Right?"

"We'll be safer if we lock down." Aldo sat down on the empty Bear Guard seat and reached a claw underneath the bank of surveillance screens. A second later, a control panel dropped down.

"What will locking down do?" Kate asked, sounding seriously impressed by her brother's command of the controls in the Lab.

"If we go into the highest-level lockdown, it will shut and lock all the doors and windows of the buildings throughout Bearhaven, for one thing. And for another, it seals the Lab. Right now, the metal is still malleable enough for approved bears and humans to go in and out, which means that it could possibly be cut through, if someone had strong enough equipment."

"Like a chain saw?" Spencer asked. Goose bumps rose on his arms as he thought back to the sounds of chain saws cutting through Bearhaven's outer wall. He knew what Aldo was still worried about.

"Right." Aldo went on, "But if we lock down, the Lab gets sealed. And it's stronger than ever that way." Aldo started to tap buttons on the control panel in front of him with his claws.

"Well, now seems like a pretty good time to go into lockdown mode, then!" Spencer said, his voice rising. The Hummer had just pulled into the clearing. It stopped beside one of the pickup trucks, and three of the doors swung open.

"I'm working on it," Aldo said, his voice as anxious as Spencer's.

Spencer watched as Margo stepped out of the driver's side door, Pam stepped out of the passenger's side, and Ivan climbed out of the backseat. Pam stared angrily at the Lab. He seemed to be barking orders, but from inside the surveillance room, Spencer, Aldo, and Kate couldn't hear him. Margo's straggly blond hair was flying out in every direction, as though she'd been running around for hours. She had a remote clutched in one hand, and a headset with a microphone clamped on her head. Ivan looked just as hulking as ever wearing a gleaming black football helmet. He strode to the back of the Hummer to get something out of the trunk.

"Aldo?" Spencer said nervously.

"I think I've almost got it," Aldo said.

"Uh-oh." Kate was apparently watching the same thing as Spencer. Ivan had pulled a chain saw out of the back of the Hummer and was heading toward the Lab. Spencer gulped. Ivan stopped a few steps away from the Lab's wall and started the chain saw.

Spencer looked from Ivan to the sharp metal teeth of the saw to Aldo, who was furiously pressing buttons on the control panel. "Aldo, do you know how to activate the lockdown?" Spencer tried not to shout, but he'd suddenly realized there was probably only one button that Aldo needed to press.

"I thought I did!" Aldo practically roared back.

"He's about to cut into the Lab!" Kate cried, her eyes glued to the screen that showed Ivan, chain saw raised.

"There!" Spencer spotted a button on top of the bank of surveillance screens. It was bright red, and set apart, it looked more important than any button on the control panel. A horrible screeching sound filled the Lab, piercing Spencer's eardrums.

"Ah!" Kate shouted. Aldo swatted at his ears with a paw.

Spencer jumped as high as he could and slammed his hand down on the button. The screeching stopped. Spencer looked back to Ivan on the screen. His biceps were bulging as he pulled on the chain saw, which was, to Spencer's surprise, stopped, stuck in the Lab's exterior wall. Spencer searched the other video feeds from inside Bearhaven. Doors and windows were swinging shut all across the valley!

"We did it!" he cried.

"*You* did it," Aldo answered, headbutting Spencer gratefully.

"Just in time, too." Kate poked her face up close to the screen where Ivan could still be seen straining to pull the chain saw free. It hadn't budged.

8

Spencer kicked a baking sheet aside as he walked into the Lab's hallway and pressed an ear against the wall. A few feet to his right, the jagged tip of the chain saw jutted into the building, frozen in place by the now-solid metal of the Lab's exterior. Kate sat next to Spencer, her head cocked to one side, focused, just like Spencer was, on hearing what was going on in the clearing a few feet away.

"Tony says the bears aren't finding anything," Margo reported in a raspy, nervous voice.

"What do you mean they aren't finding anything?" Pam screamed back at her.

"Our bears can't get into any of the buildings now," Margo started to explain, then interrupted herself with a round of hacking coughs. "Everything's locked up," she went on eventually. "But Tony says our bears aren't trying to get into the buildings anyway, which means they aren't smelling other bears inside," Margo rambled anxiously. "And there aren't any bears other than ours outside."

"Where are they, then?" Again, Pam's question came out in a furious high-pitched cry.

"Well, two of them are in there." Spencer guessed Margo was motioning toward the Lab.

"TWO BEARS?! I DID NOT COME HERE FOR ONLY TWO BEARS!" Pam screeched.

"Maybe more are in there with them." Ivan's deep voice rumbled. Spencer cringed, bracing himself for Margo to yell at Ivan to be quiet, but instead, she agreed with him.

"Ivan's right—maybe there are more bears in this place. Maybe they're all hiding in there. Or maybe Evarita *Liptrot* warned them we were coming!" Margo hurried on, trying desperately to find a way to redirect Pam's anger.

At the sound of Evarita's name, Spencer pressed his ear even harder against the Lab's wall. *What does she mean, maybe Evarita warned us?*

"She couldn't possibly have warned them. We've had her locked up for a week now," Pam spat back.

"Locked up!" Kate whispered, wide-eyed. She shuddered.

"That explains why the messages she sent were all wrong!" Spencer whispered back. "Pam used Evarita to trick us!"

"I'm going to go tell Aldo!" Kate scrambled away from the wall. Spencer watched her run toward the surveillance room, where Aldo was standing guard. He pushed the thought of Evarita as Pam's captive out of his mind—they'd have to deal with that later—and pressed his ear back up against the wall.

In the minute or so that Spencer had stopped listening to the scene outside, everything had changed. Rather than yelling, Pam had started giving orders, his voice sweet and sinister at the same time.

"—and have all the bears retreat. Get them into their

rows on the hilltop. The guards will stay. Tell them to get their blowtorches out," Pam's singsongy voice continued. "We're going to burn the place down."

Spencer's breath caught in his throat as he listened, starting to panic. *Can the Lab burn?*

"It seems to be made of some special metal," Margo croaked, echoing Spencer's thoughts. "I'm not sure it will burn."

"Not just *this* place!" Pam snapped. "All of it."

No! Spencer clenched his fists and squeezed his eyes shut. Pam couldn't mean that! He couldn't burn Bearhaven down!

"All the buildings. Everything," Pam went on. "If any bears are hiding, the fire will drive them out into the open." Cheerfulness had crept back into Pam's voice, and every word made Spencer's stomach twist. Pam was serious. "And if they really aren't here, we'll still get to watch the place go up in flames." Pam laughed, his mood obviously restored by the idea of torching Bearhaven.

"All right, I'll give the order—" Margo coughed.

"Spencer!" Kate called. "Margo is doing something with the remote!"

Spencer turned and ran to meet Kate, whose head was poking out into the hallway.

"She's having the bears retreat," he said as soon as he'd entered the surveillance room. He and Kate rushed over to stand on either side of Aldo. "Look." He pointed at the video feed of Bearhaven's center. Microchipped bears were running on all fours, appearing from every direction, heading for the hill.

"Finally!" Kate cheered.

"Spencer, what are those?" Aldo asked, nodding at the screen that showed the clearing just outside. The guards were taking turns laying their tranquilizer guns down in a metal box in the back of the trucks and pulling something else out.

"Blowtorches," Spencer said, his voice shaking a little. Bearhaven had been Kate and Aldo's only home, and Spencer had come to love it himself over the few weeks he'd been here. Evacuating had been really hard for most of the bears. After all, for many of them, it was the first place they'd ever felt safe. It had been hard for Mom and Dad, too. They'd helped to create Bearhaven, and they'd been rescuing and bringing bears here for Spencer's entire life, even though he'd only found out about that recently. Still, Spencer didn't think anyone had ever imagined Bearhaven being destroyed, even if it was abandoned. "They're going to set Bearhaven on fire," he said.

"What?!" Kate cried.

"What do you mean?" Aldo demanded, rising onto his hind legs.

"Pam gave the orders to burn everything down," Spencer said. "He thinks it will make any bears that are hiding come out. And he's mad that his team hasn't captured any of our bears yet."

"What are we going to do?!" Kate exclaimed, sounding panicked.

Aldo dropped heavily back to all fours. He moved toward the door, but Spencer stepped into the doorway, blocking Aldo's path.

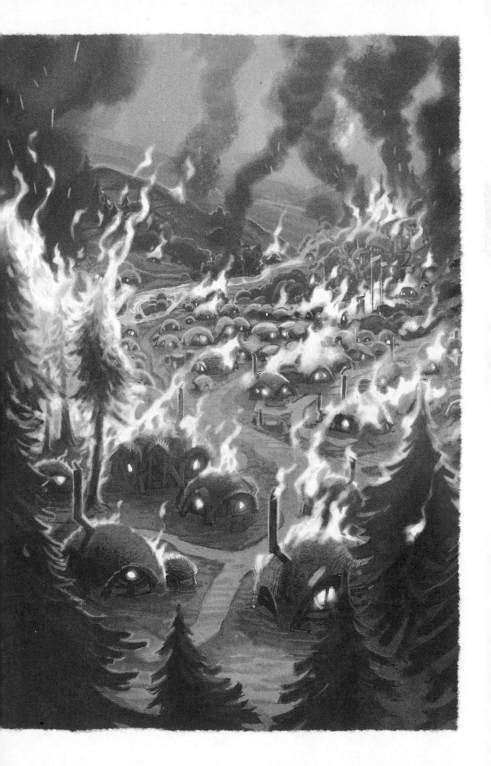

"What are you doing?" Aldo growled. "We have to stop them!"

"We can't." Spencer tried to make himself seem as big as possible. "Going out there now will just get us captured."

"I can't just sit here and watch them burn Bearhaven down!" Aldo took a step closer to Spencer, but Spencer held his ground.

"What will you do?" he challenged Aldo.

Aldo's eyes flashed with anger. The bear rose onto his hind legs, towering over Spencer. "Whatever I have to."

"That's not a good enough plan, Aldo, and you know it!" Spencer shot back. "I'm not going to let you go out there and get yourself captured!"

"You don't have to *let* me do anything! This is our *home*!" Aldo snarled. "And I took an oath to the Bear Guard to protect it. No matter what." With that, Aldo dropped back to all fours and took another threatening step toward Spencer. Spencer gulped. Would Aldo really hurt him? Spencer and Aldo had never fought before.

"Leaving the Lab now is exactly what Pam wants us to do," Spencer said, then braced himself for the bear's reaction.

"Aldo!" Kate ran over, tripping over her paws. She wedged herself between them, forcing Aldo to take a step backward. "Maybe Spencer's right! It's too dangerous to go out there now. Pam will get you if you do!"

"They're going to burn down our house!" Aldo protested, though his voice had lost some of its edge.

"A house is not worth getting captured for," Kate answered. "Trust me, I *know*."

"We need you in the Lab, Aldo," Spencer pressed. "With us."

Aldo's eyes flicked back and forth between Spencer and Kate. Spencer took a deep breath. He knew that if Aldo still wanted to leave the Lab, there wasn't much he or Kate could do to stop the full-grown bear. But after a second, Aldo huffed, then turned around and stomped back over to the bank of surveillance screens. Kate padded tentatively along behind him, before settling herself back on her haunches by his side.

Spencer went to join them. "I'm sorry, Aldo," he said quietly, breaking the tense silence.

"It's not your fault, little man," Aldo answered without taking his eyes off the surveillance screens. "It's his."

Spencer followed Aldo's gaze.

The black Hummer had returned to the hilltop overlooking Bearhaven, and Pam had returned to his perch on its hood. With an awful, creepy smile, Pam was watching his guards move through Bearhaven in their pickup trucks, setting fire to every building that would burn. Every building except for the Lab.

9

This is bad, Spencer thought as he sat in front of the bank of video screens, rolling his black jade bear figurine back and forth in his palm. The jade bear had been a gift from Mom and Dad, and it had helped him to feel stronger, and braver, in lots of tough situations over the past few weeks, but it wasn't helping him feel any better now. Then again, Spencer didn't think there was anything on earth that could possibly make him feel better about watching Bearhaven burn down.

"They're leaving!" Kate exclaimed, making Spencer jump. She and Aldo were on either side of him, watching the same terrible thing he was.

"That was fast," Spencer said. Pam's guards had only just finished torching the buildings at the center of Bearhaven.

"They must have decided if there were bears here, they'd have been smoked out by now. They don't know we're still in here." As he spoke, Aldo's eyes went back to the parts of Bearhaven that had been burning for longer—the school building, and the bears' homes.

"At least they're leaving." Spencer watched with gritted

teeth as Pam's bear army turned and marched out of view. The Hummer spun around and then accelerated away to take the lead, and the pickup trucks pulled out last. Spencer was definitely not sorry to see them go.

"Hey!" Kate said, stumbling back a few steps, as though startled. "There's someone in the fire!"

"What?!" Spencer jumped out of his seat, and started to scan the screens. Most of them were filled with the same blazing orange flames. "Where?"

"At Pinky's!" Kate shouted.

"There!" Aldo lunged forward, jutting his snout toward the screen that showed Pinky's Rehab Center and Salon. The building, like all the others in Bearhaven, was burning, but a bear was sprawled across its front steps, like it had been injured in the mayhem of Pam's army's attack.

"Who is it?" Spencer didn't recognize the bear.

"I don't know, but whoever it is, they look hurt," Aldo said.

"That bear will catch on fire!" Kate cried. "We have to do something!"

"I'll go," Aldo volunteered immediately. "I'll bring whoever it is back here."

"I'll go with you," Spencer said, trying to ignore the fact that the entire valley looked like it was burning right now. "You'll need help."

"Me too!" Kate chimed in.

"Someone has to stay here and be on surveillance duty," Aldo answered quickly.

Spencer and Kate exchanged a look.

"Kate, can you stay?" Aldo asked, making the decision

for them. "I may need Spencer's hands. And you'll be safer in here."

The cub's ears drooped. "I can stay," she said quietly.

"Your job is just as important as ours," Aldo assured her. "If Pam comes back while we're out there, we'll need someone watching who can warn us." Aldo cast one more glance at the bear in front of Pinky's, then turned to leave. "Come on, Spencer, we'll need some equipment."

Spencer and Kate followed as Aldo turned down a hallway Spencer had never seen before and ran until he reached a set of double doors. A panel of the pitted metal that made up the exterior of the Lab was attached to the wall to the left of the doors. Aldo huffed a breath of air on the panel and the doors slid open, revealing one of the coolest rooms Spencer had ever seen.

"What is this place?" Kate asked in awe.

"The Bear Guard supply closet," Aldo answered, leading the way in. Either side of the room was lined with floor to ceiling shelves, and each shelf was loaded with bear-sized security and operative gear.

"We're just leaving all of this behind? When we move to the new Bearhaven?" Spencer asked as he did a lap around the huge closet to check out all the equipment.

"No," Aldo answered. He started to pull items off shelves and pile them in the middle of the floor. "Protecting these supplies was one of the main reasons for adding the hologram to hide the Lab."

"What do you mean?" Kate asked, sniffing a big silver canister labeled "fog."

"The Plains are coming back for all our equipment. Once the danger has passed."

Spencer reached the back wall of the closet, where a single trunk stood. He lifted the top of the trunk. Bearhaven's two flags were inside. He swallowed hard at the sight of them, thinking about what was happening right now to the valley they'd flown over for so many years.

"All right," Aldo said. "We're ready."

Spencer let the trunk's lid fall shut and rushed to join Aldo and Kate by the pile of supplies. He crouched down beside it and immediately spotted what looked like a snout cover and some things that reminded him of fire extinguishers. *Of course the Bear Guard is equipped to deal with fires,* he realized with relief. They lived in the middle of a forest. If a fire broke out, they'd have to be able to do something to protect Bearhaven.

Aldo grabbed the snout cover from the pile with his mouth, then used his claws to get it into position.

"What's that for?" Kate asked.

"It's so I can breathe through the smoke outside," Aldo answered quickly. "Spencer, I didn't find anything like it for humans . . ."

Spencer scanned the shelves and spotted a big blanket. "That's okay," he said as he grabbed the pocketknife from his mission pack. He hacked off a large corner of the blanket, then wrapped it around his face and tied the two ends behind his head. He felt like a bandit in the old Western movies with a bandanna covering his nose and mouth.

In the meantime, Aldo attached two of the fire

extinguisher–looking things to his front legs. They clipped right onto the silver cuffs he always wore there to mark him as a member of the Bear Guard. There was one more on the floor between them. Spencer picked it up.

"How does this work?" he asked. The red metal cylinder had a spout on one end and a big metal button on the other.

Aldo lifted one of his front legs so that the spout was pointing out over his cuff, and paw, aiming straight ahead of him at Spencer. "See this metal button?" the bear said, tapping the button gently with his covered snout. "If I were to press it right now, you would be covered in a special foam that puts out fire."

"Got it." Spencer swung his mission pack off his back and stuffed the fire extinguisher inside.

"Kate, you know how to get in touch with us if you see something?" Aldo asked, heading for the door.

"The yellow button on my BEAR-COM," Kate answered right away. Spencer could tell she was going to take her job standing guard very seriously.

"We should check the surveillance one more time before we go, Aldo," Spencer said, breaking into a jog as soon as he'd stepped out of the Bear Guard supply closet.

"And we have to lift the lockdown mode so we can get out of here," Aldo answered, catching up. "But the faster we get to Pinky's the better that bear's chances are of surviving. Whoever it is."

10

Spencer held tight to Aldo's back as they raced through Bearhaven to Pinky's. He wished he could cover his ears. The air was hot and thick with smoke, but worse than that was the sound of buildings burning. It was as though one continuous clap of thunder was rolling over the valley.

When they reached Bearhaven's center, Aldo sprinted down the path between what used to be Raymond's Café and the meetinghouse, then turned into the clearing.

"We're surrounded!" Spencer shouted, terrified by the sight. Raymond's was burning behind them, to their right the meetinghouse was engulfed in flames, and to their left was Pinky's, its windows filled with enormous licks of fire, its roof reduced to billows of pitch-black smoke. The sun was setting, but now that they'd entered the ring of burning buildings, the sky was impossible to see through the smoke. Spencer knew the wide dirt path they'd taken to get here wouldn't burn; otherwise he would have been sure they were trapped.

"We won't be here long!" Aldo yelled back, heading straight for Pinky's. The bear was still there on the front steps, dangerously close to the burning building. The temperature rose as Spencer and Aldo got closer.

"Stay here!" Aldo shouted over the roar of flames as soon as Spencer had jumped off his back. Aldo ran up the steps on all fours, then rose onto his hind legs. A second later, a blast of fire extinguishing foam hit the doorway just behind the injured bear.

"Aldo, be careful!" Spencer yelled at the top of his lungs. The foam had missed the top of the door frame, and the fire had begun to blaze back toward Aldo and the injured bear. Aldo didn't seem to hear Spencer, though. He was already removing his snout protector and leaning over the bear on the steps. Spencer's eyes flew to the door frame again. If he didn't do something, the fire would reach the bears any minute!

"Aldo!" he screamed. The bear locked eyes with Spencer. "DUCK!" Aldo crouched low just as the first flame blazed out over his head. "Stay down!" Spencer cried. He tore the mission pack off his back and grabbed for his fire extinguisher, then vaulted up the steps until he was standing beside Aldo, his face turned away from the pummeling heat. *Here goes nothing!* he thought, and aimed his fire extinguisher at the door frame, slamming his hand down on the silver button. Foam blasted out, dousing the burning wood.

"Let's get out of here!" He tossed the empty fire extinguisher aside.

Aldo bent low over the injured bear and grabbed it by the scruff of its neck with his mouth. He started to pull the bear down the stairs. Spencer took hold of one of the unconscious bear's legs. Together, they dragged the bear away from Pinky's, pulling it to the middle of the clearing, as far away from all the burning buildings as they could get.

"She's bleeding!" Aldo shouted once he'd released the bear from his mouth. Spencer looked back to the stone steps up to Pinky's front door.

CRACK! The door frame that he'd just stopped from burning broke in two and collapsed onto the steps. Spencer looked away. *That was too close.*

"How are we going to get her to the Lab?" Aldo yelled. "She's not waking up!"

Spencer looked around wildly. Why hadn't they thought of that earlier? Everything here was on fire! He knew Pinky had bear-sized stretchers with wheels, but they were probably charred by now, and impossible to get to through the flames. They had to get out of here before the fires got worse, but what were they going to do without a cart? "Aldo!" he yelled, remembering the one other thing on wheels he'd seen in Bearhaven. "Ask Kate if Raymond's garden is on fire."

"What?" Aldo called back, confused.

"Just ask her!" Spencer shouted.

Aldo lifted a claw to his BEAR-COM and pressed the yellow button. "Kate," he yelled, "is Raymond's garden burning?"

"No!" Kate's voice answered right away.

"Kate," Spencer called, "can you see Raymond's garden cart there?"

"Yes!" Kate's voice rang out over the sound of the thundering fires.

"That's perfect!" Aldo shouted, realizing what Spencer was thinking. Raymond's massive vegetable garden was set back behind the restaurant, and in order to bring the vegetables in, Raymond piled them into a big wooden cart, and pulled them to the kitchen. "Stay with her! I'm going to get it!" Before Spencer could reply, Aldo was gone.

Spencer crouched down beside the bear to wait. He kept his eyes on her, trying to block out the thought of the fires raging all around them. Her fur was black and brown, just like Aldo's, but she wasn't as big as Aldo. *She's probably just as strong, though,* he thought, imagining all the training Pam had put her through.

Spencer felt something cold on the back of his neck. Startled, he spun around, but there was nothing behind him. He felt it again, but this time, on his forehead, then again on his cheek just above his makeshift bandanna. He looked up at the black smoke filling the sky only to be hit square in the eyeball by a fat, chilly raindrop.

"It's raining," he said aloud to himself, grateful for the cold, wet drops on his hot skin. But by the time the words had left his lips, it was pouring. The downpour was so heavy, Spencer didn't see Aldo running toward him until the bear was only a few paces away. Aldo had Raymond's cart behind him, his head through the harness that Raymond used to pull it. Aldo stepped out of the cart's harness and up to Spencer's side. "On the count of three, we lift her in!" Spencer shouted. Aldo nodded and leaned his head down over the bear. Spencer wiped rain out of his eyes, then hooked an arm under one of her legs. "ONE! TWO! THREE!"

Spencer grunted, lifting as much of the bear's weight as he could manage. Beside him, Aldo had the bear by the back of her neck as they worked to pull and lift her into the cart.

"Let's go!" Aldo called as soon as they'd settled the unconscious bear. Aldo gave a great shake of his fur and pushed his snout cover back into place. He stepped back into the cart's harness and started to pull.

Spencer ran along beside the cart, keeping an eye on the bear inside. He hadn't forgotten that she was microchipped, and conscious or not, part of Pam's army. But as the rain beat down on all of them, Spencer was distracted from the danger the injured bear could pose to them by the discovery that she wasn't black and brown at all. Instead, her fur was a rusty shade of brown. The black had been smoke, or ashes from the fire, and by now, the rain had washed it away.

11

Spencer pushed Ivan's abandoned chain saw away from the opening in the side of the Lab to make space for Aldo and Raymond's garden cart. The rain hadn't let up, but Spencer was glad for the shower. He could feel the sweat and soot from the rescue mission washing off him, and he hoped the rain would at least slow down the fires that still raged throughout the valley.

"Almost there!" he called back to Aldo, who was just a few paces away but moving slowly now that they'd reached the dark clearing around the Lab. Spencer could tell that pulling a grown bear through heavy rain and smoke had been harder than Aldo had imagined, and after narrowly escaping capture by Pam's army earlier, the bear was exhausted. Aldo didn't answer, but a few heavy steps later, he was crossing into the brightly lit Lab. Once the cart was inside, Spencer followed and let the special metal seal shut behind them.

"Aldo! Spencer!" Kate's voice rang through the hallway. A moment later, the cub appeared, running to meet them. "How's the—" she started, only to hit the large puddle that was pooling around Aldo and the cart. Her legs flew out from under her, and she slid on her belly straight into the wall. "It's raining!" she said, scrambling to her feet as though nothing had happened. "Really hard."

Spencer laughed, wringing out the front of his T-shirt. "We know."

"How's the bear?" Kate asked, trotting a little more carefully back over to the cart.

"She's hurt," Aldo said. "We should see what we can do for her injury." He started to move again, but instead of returning to the surveillance room, he led the way to Professor Weaver's workshop. Spencer had been inside this room before. It was the reason the Lab was named the Lab: because it was the state-of-the-art laboratory where Professor Weaver created all of Bearhaven's cool technology, like the BEAR-COMs and the holograms that they used for security. Spencer turned on the lights as they entered the room, revealing silver tables with robotic, human-looking hands poised above them.

Aldo pulled Raymond's cart out into the center of the room and then stepped out of the harness. He joined Spencer and Kate at the back of the cart.

"She's breathing, so that's good," Spencer said, looking down at the soaking wet, unconscious bear in the cart. With her rusty-brown fur slicked flat against her body, and her legs tucked in around her, the bear didn't look nearly as big and threatening as the bears that had chased Spencer, Aldo, and Kate, but Spencer couldn't let himself forget she was still one of them. "We'd better get her out of the cart so we can see where she's bleeding from," he said.

"Hold on," Aldo said. "We can't just drop her on the

floor. And we're going to need supplies to clean the wound. Spencer, see what you have in your mission pack, and, Kate, come with me." With that, the two bears rushed out of the room. Spencer saw Aldo pause in the hallway and give a great shake of his fur, showering water everywhere, before continuing, Spencer guessed, to the Bear Guard supply closet.

Spencer slipped off his backpack and stepped over to one of the silver tables. His wet sneakers squeaked and sloshed, and Spencer shivered, wishing he had a dry set of clothes in his mission pack. A couple of peanut butter sandwiches would be nice, too. He pushed the thoughts of clothes and food from his mind. There was an injured bear six feet away who was in much worse shape than he was.

He unzipped his mission pack and shook the contents out onto the silver table. He couldn't resist grabbing a Raymond's fuel bar and starting to eat as he sifted through the rest of the pile. He pulled out a knob of ginger root, the bears' natural painkiller, then his travel first aid kit and a flashlight.

Spencer was just taking the last bite of his fuel bar when Aldo and Kate returned, each dragging a blanket that looked like it had supplies bundled inside. When they reached the middle of the room, they dropped their blankets, which unrolled to reveal their contents. Spencer spotted a BEAR-COM, more fuel bars, a variety of bandages, and a bundle of gray fabric.

"Spencer, look what we found for you!" Kate said,

diving into the pile and nudging the gray bundle toward Spencer. "Clothes!" she exclaimed as Spencer realized that the bundle was actually a pair of sweatpants and a sweatshirt all balled up.

He grabbed the sweats and headed for the door. "Where did these come from?"

"They were in the supply closet," Aldo said distractedly as he pushed the supplies off his blanket and onto the floor beside it. "Mark or your dad must have left them there sometime."

"Well, thanks!" Spencer stepped out into the hallway and quickly peeled off his sopping wet clothes, replacing them with the sweatpants and sweatshirt. "That's better," he said as he rolled up the sleeves of the adult-sized sweatshirt. He jogged back into the lab, barefoot, but now in dry clothes, to find that Aldo and Kate were just moving the injured bear from the cart to one of the blankets on the floor.

"How's she doing?" he asked, going to kneel beside them.

"Doesn't look like anything's changed," Aldo answered.

"Well, there's the problem." Spencer pointed as he leaned closer to the bear. The back of her head had a huge gash in it. "I think I should clean out the wound." Kate scooted over to the silver table where Spencer had unloaded his mission pack and grabbed the travel first aid kit in her mouth. "Thanks," Spencer said, taking it from her. He flipped it open and pulled out all the sterilizing cloths, then set to work.

"I wonder how she got hurt," Aldo said, passing Kate a

fuel bar from a pile beside him. He and Kate started to eat as Spencer worked.

"I don't know," Spencer answered. "But I can't believe Pam left her behind like that. The guards had to have seen her when they set the building on fire."

"She would've died if it wasn't for us!" Kate chimed in.

Aldo nodded thoughtfully. "It looks like it's bleeding more, Spencer," he said.

"I think it is." Spencer sat back, adding one more sterilizing cloth to a bloody pile beside him. "It's really deep . . . and I can't see what's wrong. Kate, can you get the flashlight from my stuff?" he asked, and a second later, the cub was holding it out to him in her mouth. Spencer clicked on the flashlight and Aldo and Kate crowded in beside him to get a good look.

"There's something shiny in there," Kate whispered.

"I see it, too," Aldo said. "But what is it?"

Spencer leaned closer. In the middle of the cut, right where it was deepest, there was a little metal thing, partly buried in the bear's flesh. "Is that what cut her?" he asked, puzzled.

"It can't be—it's too small." Aldo sat back on his haunches. "But what else would be stuck in a bear's head like that?"

"A microchip!" Spencer exclaimed, thinking of the one thing he knew for sure was in this bear's head. "That's what it has to be!"

"What do we do?" Kate cried, as though just seeing a microchip could somehow hurt them.

"We take it out." Spencer found a pair of tweezers in his kit. "Aldo, can you hold the flashlight?" he asked. Aldo took the flashlight from Spencer and held it between his teeth, pointing down over the bear's head. "When she wakes up, she won't be dangerous to us! Pam won't be able to control her anymore," Spencer explained.

He zeroed his focus in on the little piece of metal. *It's just like taking out a splinter,* he told himself as a wave of queasiness washed over him. Spencer reached the tweezers into the bear's wound and grabbed hold of the microchip. With a little tug, it came free. He held it up close to the flashlight. It was the size of a dime.

"How can something that small be so dangerous?" Aldo wondered aloud.

Spencer looked down at the open wound on the back of the unconscious bear's head, and suddenly became furious. Not only was Pam abusing bears in a hundred different ways, the worst one being controlling their minds and bodies with microchips, but he cared so little about his bears that he would leave one behind to die!

"Now what?" Kate asked quietly, her eyes locked on the microchip.

"Now we destroy it." Spencer got to his feet and grabbed a hammer from his pile of supplies. He stomped over to an empty silver table and set the microchip down in the middle of it. "Pam thinks he's so powerful," Spencer said. "But we're going to show him. You don't"—*bang!* Spencer slammed the hammer down on the microchip—"mess"—*bang!*—"with Bearhaven." He set the hammer down on top of the tiny pile of metal rubble he'd quickly reduced the microchip to and turned around.

Aldo and Kate were staring at him, wide eyed.

"Uh . . . is it destroyed?" Kate asked tentatively.

"Yup." Spencer felt much better. "Let's bandage her up," he said cheerfully.

12

Spencer woke up on the floor of the Lab. He was wrapped in a blanket, his head resting on Kate's back. By the way the cub's breath was whistling in and out of her mouth, he could tell she was still asleep. He looked over at Aldo and was surprised to find that he was sleeping, too.

Spencer quickly scrambled to a seat and turned around. The blanket where the injured bear had been lying was empty.

"Aldo! Kate!" Spencer whispered. "Wake up!"

Aldo woke with a start. "Oh no," he grumbled as soon as his eyes landed on the empty blanket. Spencer, Aldo, and Kate had been taking turns through the night, keeping watch over the injured bear. "I fell asleep on my watch," Aldo said, getting to all fours.

"What's going on?" Kate asked groggily as she stretched.

"The bear is gone." Spencer got to his feet.

"We'd better go find her," Aldo said. "But we have to be careful. She's probably in pain and confused. There's no telling how she'll respond to seeing us."

Spencer nodded. He also knew what Aldo hadn't said: that even without her microchip, the strange bear could be dangerous. He grabbed the BEAR-COM that Aldo and Kate had brought from the supply closet and the knob of ginger from his mission pack and stuffed them into the pockets of his sweatpants. "Let's go," he said.

It didn't take them long to find the bear. As soon as they stepped out of Professor Weaver's workshop, the grunting and banging sounds led them right to her. She was in the surveillance room. Spencer, Aldo, and Kate crept up to the door and poked their heads around the edge.

"She's going to be in big trouble," Kate whispered.

The room was destroyed. The bank of surveillance screens looked like someone had attacked it with a sledgehammer, and the control panel was broken in half, its parts tossed to two corners of the room.

The grunting and banging continued. Spencer craned his neck around the door frame to the other half of the room. The bear was clawing and swatting at the section of floor that Spencer knew to be a secret entrance to the council room.

The Bear Council was the group of bears plus Spencer's parents and his uncle Mark that made the most important decisions for Bearhaven. The Lab was their headquarters, too, but Spencer couldn't imagine how one of Pam's bears would know where their private meetings were held.

"Why is she doing that?" Kate asked in a whisper. The bear inside the surveillance room froze, her back to the doorway. Aldo stepped in front of Spencer and Kate, shielding them. The bear in the room slowly turned. She locked eyes with Aldo and stared him down.

Pop! Pop!

"We don't mean—" Aldo started, but didn't have the chance to finish before the bear charged him. He rose onto his hind legs just as she reached him. She rose into the same position, huffing, her eyes full of fury. She swatted at Aldo, who blocked the attack. Spencer flinched and stepped back into the hallway, pushing Kate with him. The bear swatted again, and this time, she grunted a string of Ragayo as she struck out at Aldo.

"You're in Bearhaven," Aldo answered, stepping backward to avoid the next blow. "You're safe," he went on, his Ragayo translating through the BEAR-COM for Spencer to understand.

The bear dropped down to all fours, though she didn't look any less angry, and she never took her eyes off Aldo's. She flashed her teeth, then grunted in Ragayo again.

"You were hurt, so we brought you here to help you," Aldo explained. The bear started to pace. She huffed and swatted the floor with a paw. "Yes, there's something under this floor," he answered her next series of grunts. "If you'll calm down—"

Pop! The bear charged him again, her jaws open. She snapped at Aldo, who stepped toward her and pushed her back. Spencer and Kate exchanged a look, shocked that Aldo would fight. "Calm down," he said, taking charge. The bear stepped back a few paces. She swatted the floor and huffed. Aldo stood his ground, staring down at her. After a few more jaw pops, huffs, and swipes at Aldo, the bear sat back on her haunches and fell silent.

"Listen to me," Aldo said, his voice steady. "You are safe with us, but you have to promise that we are safe with you.

If you do that and agree to wear something around your neck to communicate the way I do, then I'll let you see what's down below."

The bear responded in Ragayo, but Spencer could tell by the way Aldo relaxed that she had agreed. He stepped aside, giving her a full view of Spencer and Kate. The bear bristled at the sight of them.

"This is Spencer Plain, and my sister, Kate," he said. "Spencer, will you give her a BEAR-COM?"

Spencer gulped and pulled the extra BEAR-COM from his pocket. "She promised she wouldn't hurt us?" he asked Aldo.

"She promised."

"Okay." Spencer slowly approached the bear. She leaned away as soon as he got close. *"Shala."* He growled the Ragayo word for "safe," trying to reassure her. Confusion flashed in the bear's eyes, but in the time that she hesitated, Spencer reached forward and with shaking hands fastened the BEAR-COM around her neck. He switched the translating device on, then stepped back to stand beside Aldo.

"Now we can all communicate," Aldo said. "I'm Aldo."

"I don't want to communicate; I want to see whatever's under this floor," the bear snapped.

Aldo ignored her. "What's your name?"

"Zoe. Now keep your promise."

Aldo shot Spencer a look, but Spencer wasn't sure what the bear meant by it. None of the Bearhaven bears he knew were named Zoe, but it sounded familiar . . .

"All right," Aldo said, interrupting Spencer's thoughts. He padded over to the wall where a secret button was camouflaged. "Everyone has to stand here." He motioned toward the silver slab on the floor that Zoe had been pounding at when they discovered her. Zoe hurried over, and Spencer and Kate moved to stand beside her.

Whoosh! Aldo hit the button, and the slab lowered through the floor only to stop half a second later in the hidden corridor below. Zoe launched herself off the platform just the way Spencer had the first time he'd come here, to demand that the council find his missing parents.

"Aldo!" Spencer exclaimed, realizing all of a sudden *why* he knew of a bear named Zoe. "We know about a bear named Zoe! Pinky had a cub named Zoe who was taken to Moon Farm and never seen again!" Spencer and Aldo had learned all about her in the council meeting about Kate's kidnapping.

"I know!" Aldo answered, taking off after Zoe, who had gone crashing through the heavy wooden doors and into the council room. "Come on!"

"What is this place?!" Kate cried, running along beside her brother.

"This is where the council meets!" Spencer answered, rushing into the room. He skidded to a halt as soon as he was inside. Zoe had overturned a chair, and her snout was buried in its cushions as though she was searching wildly for something that may have been left there. Spencer looked around the council table. Each member had a designated seat. The one Zoe was furiously rooting through was Pinky's.

13

"Where is my mother?" Zoe sat back on her haunches beside Pinky's overturned chair in the council room. Her voice was quiet, all the edge suddenly gone, as she looked back and forth from Spencer, to Aldo, to Kate, who stood watching from just inside the doorway.

"Is Pinky . . . your mother?" Spencer asked back. He wanted to believe that they had found Pinky's long-lost cub. But was it really possible?!

"Yes," Zoe answered, her fur bristling with excitement. "I smelled her before, too. When we were ordered to search for bears. I smelled her in a building—"

"Pinky's Rehab Center and Salon," Aldo said. "That's where we found you."

"The door was open, and I was trying to get to her," Zoe explained. "I don't know what happened after that." Zoe bent her bandaged head over Pinky's chair again, and Spencer suddenly realized how she had gotten hurt. He must have activated the lockdown just as Zoe tried to get into Pinky's to find her mother, and the door swung shut on her. "The next thing I knew, I was in this building with you three, and I smelled her again. I can smell her now,"

Zoe went on, her tone turning urgent. "Where is she? I have to see her!"

"She's in the woods," Spencer answered. "Not far from here."

"She's hiding with the rest of our bears!" Kate piped up.

"Kate!" Aldo said, shooting her a warning look.

"Don't worry, I'm not going to report back. I'm never *going* back." Zoe quickly padded over to where Spencer, Aldo, and Kate were standing. "You can trust me, I promise. I stopped hoping to ever see my mom again so long ago. I never knew she was in Bearhaven. If you take me to her, I'll help you however I can."

"See," Kate muttered, glaring at Aldo. "We can trust her."

"I'm sorry if I was a little . . . unfriendly earlier. I was so confused," Zoe added, looking at Aldo. "But if my mom and the rest of your bears are in the woods, we should go now," Zoe hurried on. "Pam won't leave the area without bears. You should tell them. It's not safe to be anywhere near here."

Spencer looked at Aldo. If Zoe was right, they should get back to their sleuth right away to warn B.D.

"Let's get ready to go, then," Aldo said, obviously thinking the same thing Spencer was.

"Do you think Mom and Dad are okay, Aldo?" Kate asked, her voice suddenly anxious. "And Lisle, and Winston, and Jo-Jo?" she listed the rest of the Weaver siblings as Spencer started to think of all the other bears they'd left hidden in the woods.

"Let's hope so," Aldo answered, heading for the door.

* * *

Spencer stepped back into the ransacked surveillance room wearing yesterday's clothes, which had dried while he was sleeping. His full mission pack was on his back, and he had seven Raymond's fuel bars and a knob of ginger root piled in his arms.

"—really sorry about this," Zoe was saying as she looked unhappily around the room. Aldo was standing in front of the surveillance screens, examining each one.

"It's okay," he said, though by the tone of his voice it didn't sound like there was anything okay about the state of Bearhaven's surveillance system.

"How does your head feel?" Spencer asked as he passed two fuel bars and the ginger to Zoe.

"It's throbbing, but Kate says my mom's a great medic," Zoe answered.

"She is!" Kate called from where she'd been sniffing at one half of the broken control panel. "She takes care of everyone who comes here hurt! She'll fix you right up!" She trotted over to get her breakfast from Spencer, who had gone to stand by Aldo's side.

"They're all down," Aldo muttered, accepting two bars. Spencer scanned the screens. Not one of them had an image on it anymore. They were useless.

"So there's no way for us to know if the coast is clear before we leave the Lab?" Spencer asked between bites of his own fuel bar. "That sounds dangerous."

"It is," Aldo agreed. "And now that there's daylight again, I wouldn't be surprised if Pam sent guards back here."

"Is there an emergency exit?" Zoe asked. Spencer shook his head, but then Aldo spoke up.

"Yes," the bear said, turning away from the broken surveillance screens.

"There is!?" Spencer and Kate asked at the same time.

"There is. I've just never heard of anyone actually using it before," Aldo answered. "But it looks like we're going to have to. Come on."

Aldo hurried back over the silver panel in the floor, and Spencer, Kate, and Zoe crowded in around him. A second later, they'd all lowered to the hidden corridor below. Aldo took off at a run toward the council room. Once he got there, he pushed a few chairs aside, then crouched down and shuffled beneath the huge wooden conference table. Kate immediately scrambled under to join her brother, and Zoe followed close behind.

Spencer pulled his flashlight out of his mission pack and crawled beneath the table to join the bears. At first, he was shocked that there was space for all of them there. Then he realized that Aldo was already gone.

"I'm next!" Kate said, and Spencer watched as she disappeared through what looked like a hole in the floor. Zoe followed, clearing the way for Spencer to finally see what was going on. Two silver panels had slid apart in the middle of the floor beneath the table, revealing a set of narrow steps that led down, deeper into the ground. Spencer shone his flashlight down into the hole. Zoe was just reaching the bottom step. She moved away, into what looked like a dimly lit hallway.

"What is this place?!" Kate's voice echoed up to Spencer.

"It's a tunnel," Aldo replied just as Spencer swung his legs into the hole in the council room floor and started down the steps. "Spencer," Aldo called when Spencer was halfway down. "There's a button right by your head. Can you press it?"

Spencer reached out to feel the wall by his head. His fingers hit tightly packed dirt, as though this tunnel had been cut directly into the earth and left unfinished. After groping around the dirt wall for a second, Spencer found a smooth button. He pressed it, and the silver panels slid shut above him, closing the secret entrance beneath the council table.

"Creepy," he said once he'd reached the bottom of the stairs. Little lights poked out of the tunnel wall, but they were far apart and didn't cast much light. Spencer was glad he had his flashlight. Spencer felt something slither across his sneaker. "Gah!" He jumped to one side, banging into Kate.

"What's wrong?!" she cried.

"Nothing," Spencer answered sheepishly. He tried to sound calm as he searched the tunnel's dirt floor with his flashlight.

"I know it's not pretty," Aldo said apologetically, looking around at the tunnel. "But it'll take us to the TUBE station without any chance of being seen."

"What's a TUBE station?" Zoe asked.

"It's where Bearhaven's train is kept." Spencer reached into his pocket for his jade bear. It wasn't that the tunnel wasn't pretty that bothered him; it was the feeling that slithery, creepy-crawly creatures were hiding in all the shadows that made him antsy.

"And it's safe? This tunnel?" Zoe eyed the roughly cut walls suspiciously.

"It should be." Aldo started to walk deeper into the tunnel, as though expecting everyone to follow. "But like I said, I'm not sure anyone's ever used it."

"Oh, great," Kate grumbled.

Aldo turned back and realized that nobody else had moved. "Well, it's safer than taking our chances with *Pam,* isn't it?" As Aldo's voice echoed into the dark behind him, a little chunk of the tunnel's rounded ceiling came loose and dropped to the dirt floor at Aldo's feet.

14

Spencer had never been so happy to see a door in his life. He, Aldo, Kate, and Zoe had run the length of the secret tunnel that served as the Lab's emergency exit without any more of the ceiling falling or any other slithering things coming out of the shadows, but even so none of them had seemed quite sure that they'd make it all the way to the TUBE station. Until they did.

"Finally!" Kate exclaimed when the tunnel ended.

"Finally," Aldo echoed. He headbutted the door open to reveal a maintenance closet filled with tools and supplies, and four or five bear-sized brooms clattered to the floor. Aldo stepped through, then immediately led the way out onto the TUBE platform.

Spencer was the last one out of the tunnel. He swung the wooden door shut behind him, happy that it looked as though there had never been a door there at all. The worn brick wall hid it completely. He rushed out to join the bears. Zoe was staring in awe at the TUBE.

"We use it for most of the bear rescue missions," Kate said proudly, as though she drove the TUBE herself.

"When you're in captivity for a long time, you hear stories about Bearhaven—how incredible it is . . . and about all the amazing things you have here . . ." Zoe said. "I just assumed most of those stories were made up."

Spencer remembered being awestruck, too, when he first saw the gleaming train with copper-colored windows, but there wasn't time to show off all the cool things about the TUBE. They had already been gone long enough and had to report back to B.D. "We'd better keep moving," Spencer said, jogging over to where Aldo was standing beside a set of elevator doors.

"You'll get to see a few more of Bearhaven's innovations on the way, though, Zoe," Aldo called, as though he didn't want to let the bear down.

"Like this elevator!" Kate said, jutting her snout toward the elevator as she and Zoe approached. "It goes up into a *tree!*"

Aldo pressed a button, and the doors slid open to reveal a hollowed-out, polished tree trunk. They all stepped inside, and the doors slid shut, closing them in darkness as the platform beneath their feet began to rise. When the doors slid open again, they'd reached the bridge in the trees. This time, Spencer could see the wide wooden planks that stretched from the tree elevator across the width of Bearhaven's outer wall.

"The hologram must have gone down when the control panel broke," Aldo said as he crouched low for Spencer to climb onto his back. As usual, there was no way Spencer would be able to climb from the bridge in the treetops to the forest floor without Aldo's help. Spencer grabbed two fistfuls of the bear's fur and swung himself onto Aldo's back.

"It's not like we have anything left to hide anyway," Spencer said. "Pam's already seen Bearhaven."

Kate and Zoe followed close behind as Aldo made his way across the bridge in the trees. When Aldo started to climb down toward the ground, Spencer could hear Zoe and Kate moving through the trees around them, finding their own routes. Zoe was the first to reach the forest floor and was waiting there when Aldo jumped down to the dirt path.

"You're fast," Aldo said, obviously impressed.

"I've been trained," Zoe answered. Spencer's stomach twisted at the reminder that Pam's bear army was just as strong and fast as Bearhaven's strongest, fastest bears. Kate jumped to the ground a few seconds later, and Aldo set off at a run, with Spencer still on his back, toward the checkpoint for sleuth number one, with Zoe and Kate behind him.

Aldo slowed to a walk when the familiar tree came into view. They hadn't seen any of Pam's guards or bears on the sprint here, but they hadn't seen any of Bearhaven's, either.

"I don't smell anyone," Aldo said quietly, so that only Spencer would hear him. Spencer squinted, searching the branches of the tree where they'd last seen Darwin, John Shirley, and B.D. "Look at the ground," the bear added, but Spencer didn't listen. Something on the tree trunk just below the lowest branch had caught his eye. "These aren't the tracks of bears marching," Aldo went on.

"Oh no," Spencer gasped. He slipped off Aldo's back

and ran up to the tree. A tranquilizer dart was stuck in the bark. He reached for it, tugging it out of the tree trunk. There was no mistaking it. One of Pam's guards had shot at this tree. Spencer looked up. He spotted half a dozen more darts, and not a single sign of Darwin, John Shirley, or B.D.

"We're too late," he whispered. Slowly, he turned around to face Aldo, Kate, and Zoe. They were all scanning the ground in silence, grim expressions on their faces. The dirt was riddled with bear tracks, boot tracks, and tire tracks. There had been a struggle here. And it was obvious Pam had won.

15

"Nobody panic," Spencer said, though he could feel himself starting to panic. He, Aldo, Kate, and Zoe had gone to each of the sixteen sleuth checkpoints, and all of them looked the same: full of Pam's army's tracks and strewn with tranquilizer darts, but not a bear in sight. At first they hadn't wanted to believe it. But now it was time to face the facts. It looked like all of Bearhaven's bears had been captured.

"I was so close to finally seeing my mom again," Zoe practically whimpered, her eyes on the ground as she pawed at the dirt.

"What are we going to do?" Kate cried.

"Well, we're not going to give up," Aldo said. Spencer could tell the bear was trying to sound brave, despite the fact that aside from Kate, his entire family was now most likely captive.

"We *can't* give up," Spencer jumped in. He knew how the bears felt—after all, his own family had been Pam's prisoners not long ago. "Think of all the times we've beaten Pam! You've *both* been Pam's captives before, and now you're free." He looked back and forth between Kate and Zoe, then went on. "Our bears aren't lost forever. We just need a plan for how to get them back."

"We have to find out where he's taken everyone," Aldo spoke up. "And what he's doing with them."

"We have to stop him from leaving here," Zoe chimed in. "Once he gets them back to Moon Farm . . ." The bear drifted off, but they'd all seen Moon Farm, Pam's horrible factory, on its creepy island before. They knew just as well as Zoe did that if Pam got all of Bearhaven's bears back there, hope really could be lost.

"We can follow the tracks," Aldo said.

"And I can smell for Mom and Dad," Kate offered.

"Great!" Spencer strode over to Aldo's side. The bear crouched down, and Spencer climbed onto his back. "Let's get moving."

Zoe spotted Pam's camp first. "There," she whispered, jutting her head toward a cluster of trees up ahead. Between the trees, Spencer could just make out Pam's Hummer. They crept closer. The Hummer was parked beside a big trailer just like the ones movie stars used when they were working on location.

Aldo cut off to the left, then chose the biggest nearby tree and started to climb. Once Aldo had settled himself in the branches, Spencer got off the bear's back. He picked a branch and scooted out onto it, trying to get a better view of Pam's camp below.

"Can you see anything, Spencer?" Kate whispered. He

could hear Aldo, Zoe, and Kate moving quietly around the branches of the tree, making their way to lookout points of their own.

"Yes," Spencer answered when he'd finally found himself a perch with a clear view. But he didn't say more. He didn't think he'd be able to get the words out.

Pam's camp was made up of a ring of vehicles. The Hummer and trailer made up the section of the ring that was closest to where Spencer hid now, and huge cargo trucks parked end to end made up the rest of it. There were five cargo trucks, and between each one there was just enough space for a pickup truck to pull through into the middle of the camp.

Pam's bear army was being marched into two of the cargo trucks. They moved robotically, in a single-file line, but that didn't surprise Spencer, because Margo was standing nearby, a remote clutched in her hand. Spencer's stomach twisted as he realized that Margo was only using two trucks, and that forty-four bears were supposed to get crammed into each vehicle. He tried not to think of all those bears smashed into tiny, dirty cages, but he knew that was exactly what was happening. He looked away, but the activity in the rest of the camp was even worse.

The pickup trucks had all been pulled into the middle of the camp. Their truck beds were full, loaded with unconscious Bearhaven bears. Spencer spotted B.D. right away. He and John Shirley were piled into the back of a truck together with a few other bears whose faces Spencer couldn't make out. None of them were moving. If it hadn't been for the awkward angles of the bears' limbs, and the fact that they were all lumped together carelessly, Spencer might have convinced himself that the bears were sleeping. B.D. almost looked peaceful.

Teams of guards were working together to move the tranquilized bears from pickup trucks to cargo trucks and, Spencer guessed, into tiny cages just like the ones the microchipped bears were filing into now. Before each Bearhaven bear was dragged to his or her new prison, their BEAR-COM was removed and added to a growing pile.

Bang! All of a sudden, the trailer door was thrown open. Pam strode out into the middle of his camp. He didn't look happy. A bear emerged from the trailer behind him. It was Dora. The jet-black bear who always stayed by Pam's side padded after him, but Spencer could see that her snout was moving rapidly. She was smelling for something. When Pam stopped beside the pile of discarded BEAR-COMs, Dora kept walking. She went directly to the truck where B.D. and John Shirley, her brothers, lay. Spencer was glad Dora's back was turned to him now. He didn't think he'd be able to stand the sight of Dora's face as she looked down at the tranquilized bears whose job it had been to protect her only cub, Darwin, and who she had come here to join in freedom.

"Ivan, when they're all in, lock the doors," Margo ordered in a rasping voice, drawing Spencer's attention away from Dora. Margo hurried over to meet Pam. When she reached him, Pam kicked the pile of BEAR-COMs, scattering Bearhaven's most prized translating technology in the dirt at his feet.

"What are these things?" he asked. "Tracking devices?"

"Definitely tracking devices," Margo answered. She kicked the pile, just like Pam had, but one of the BEAR-COMs looped around her ankle and got stuck. Pam shot Margo a nasty look as she awkwardly shook the BEAR-COM off her leg.

"Why did only eighty-seven of my bears come back to camp?" Pam demanded. Spencer gulped. Pam was referring to his missing eighty-eighth bear—Zoe.

"One got hurt in Bearhaven—a head wound," Margo replied anxiously. "It would've taken too much work to get her out in the middle of the fire, just for her to die in an hour or two."

"I see." Pam's voice was dangerously sweet as he stared Margo down. "Don't let it happen again," he snapped after a second. "Or you'll pay for the lost bear yourself." Pam turned his attention to the activity in the camp, and Spencer relaxed a tiny bit. As far as Pam was concerned, Zoe was long dead by now.

Margo jerked her head at the cluster of pickup trucks filled with tranquilized bears. "We captured seventy-two bears today. This is the last load."

"And my cub?" Pam asked as he scanned the trucks. Margo shook her head. She looked nervous again. "Seventy-two bears and not one of them is my cub?" Pam shrieked. Out of the corner of his eye, Spencer saw Dora's ears twitch at the sound of Pam's high-pitched voice.

"He doesn't have Darwin!" Spencer whispered, wishing Dora could hear and understand him now, too. She was patrolling the pickup trucks, searching, Spencer was sure, for her cub.

"If he only has seventy-two bears, Darwin's not the only one who escaped!" Aldo whispered back from somewhere higher in the tree. "There were seventy-nine Bearhaven bears in the woods yesterday, including me and Kate."

"Nobody leaves here until we have Darwin," Pam hollered at the top of his lungs. All the guards stopped what they were doing to listen. "And every bear I already sold at the Hidden Rock Zoo auction had better be in those trucks. Because we are not leaving without them, either." Pam kicked the BEAR-COMs again. "And get this junk out of my way!" He stormed back to his trailer and slammed the door. The camp fell silent in his wake.

Spencer took a deep breath. He wanted to feel relieved. Pam's army wasn't leaving for Moon Farm yet. Which meant there was still a chance to rescue the Bearhaven bears Pam had already tranquilized and locked up. But Pam had just sworn he wouldn't leave until he'd captured Darwin and all the bears he'd already sold to greedy animal dealers at an auction two weeks ago. And Aldo and Kate were two of those bears.

16

"If Pam has seventy-two bears, and me and Aldo are still free," Kate said as they made their way back to their sleuth's checkpoint, "that means *five* of our bears are still out here somewhere!"

"Darwin is one of the five," Spencer said, searching the tree trunks as they walked. He couldn't believe how lucky they were that Darwin had escaped. As long as Pam didn't have Darwin, Bearhaven's bears wouldn't be carted off to Moon Farm and sold to a million different people and scattered to a million different places. And Dora would still uphold the deal she'd made with Spencer and Aldo when they rescued Darwin: to pretend to be loyal to Pam until finally helping Bearhaven to defeat him. "But that leaves four bears. We don't know which bears they are, and they could be anywhere."

"We'll find them," Aldo said. "Just keep looking."

"Can you tell me just one more time what exactly we're looking for," Zoe asked. "Sorry, it's just that I don't have a ton of experience with real trees . . . that have real bark."

"It's okay," Spencer said, trying to make Zoe feel better about her lack of experience in the wild. "I had to learn the system, too, a few days ago."

"We're looking for a tree with an X on the trunk," Aldo explained patiently as they continued to move through the woods. "In an emergency, Bearhaven bears were supposed to get as close to the checkpoint for sleuth number one as possible, and hide. They should have left claw marks on the trunk of the tree they're hiding in so we would know where to find them."

"Like that!" Kate shouted. Spencer rushed after the cub as she raced up to a tree not far from the first sleuth checkpoint. There were claw marks across its bark. They roughly made the shape of an X, though at a glance, it would just look like a bear had sharpened their claws here in passing.

"That's it!" he exclaimed, running up to the claw marked tree.

"Spencer! Kate!" a cub's voice called. It wasn't Darwin, the cub Spencer had expected.

"Quiet, Kenny," another voice drifted down.

"Ro Ro!" Spencer called. He was happy to discover that the mother bear and her cubs had escaped a second capture by Pam, though he couldn't help feeling a quick flash of disappointment that it wasn't Darwin who had called down to them.

"Let's go up there," Aldo said, padding up to Spencer's side. "It's safer if we all talk in the tree." Kate rushed over and scrambled up into the tree. Aldo followed her.

"Go ahead, Zoe," Spencer said. He turned around to find that Zoe hadn't come any closer. She sat back on her hind legs, looking at him. "What's wrong?"

"I was hoping it was going to be my mom," Zoe answered quietly. "I know that's selfish . . . but I can't help it."

"Maybe the next bear we find will be," Spencer said. "Come on, come meet Ro Ro. She belonged to Pam once, too. But I helped to rescue her, and your mom took care of her when she got to Bearhaven."

Zoe seemed to perk up at hearing that Ro Ro knew Pinky. "All right." She trotted over, and a second later, she'd expertly climbed up into the tree. Spencer followed, much more slowly. He pulled himself up over the lowest branch only to have a black bundle of fur nearly knock him back to the ground.

Spencer resisted the urge to shout as he grabbed for something to hold on to. His hands only hit air. Just as he started to tip backward out of the tree, he felt a bear's jaws clamp onto his mission pack, stopping him from falling. Spencer wrapped his arms around Darwin, who he'd just now realized was the black furry bundle clinging to his chest, and allowed himself to be tugged onto a steady seat on a tree branch by the bear above him.

"Darwin," Marguerite gently scolded the cub. "You have to be more careful."

"Spencer!" the little cub cried. "Uncle B.D. and Uncle John Shirley—they got taken away!"

"I know." Spencer hugged the cub. "But we're going to get them back."

The silvery, almost iridescent fur on Darwin's chest

caught Spencer's eye as the cub peered up at him. Darwin was jet-black, except for a shining blaze mark in the perfect shape of a crown. Spencer didn't know what, aside from that regal blaze mark, made the cub so valuable to Pam, but he knew they were lucky Pam hadn't captured Darwin in his first attack.

"Where's Winnie?" Kate asked, interrupting Spencer's thoughts.

Spencer looked around the tree. Marguerite was a few branches above him. Spencer rarely saw the large, sleek bear outside the TUBE, where she could usually be found in her attendant uniform, preparing the train and its passengers for the next mission. He was glad she was here now, though. A little higher up, perched in the crook of a wide branch and the tree trunk, were Ro Ro and Kenny, but Ro Ro's other cub, Kenny's sister Winnie, didn't seem to be here.

"She got caught," Kenny answered, then buried his face in Ro Ro's fur.

"I'm sorry . . ." Spencer whispered.

"Have you seen anyone else?" Aldo changed the subject quickly. "Since the attack?" Without Winnie, there were only four bears here, which meant Bearhaven still had one free.

"Raymond," Ro Ro answered. "He's—"

"I'm here," the bear called. Spencer looked down. Raymond was just beginning to climb the tree's trunk. He had four trout in his mouth, which he passed to Marguerite as soon as he was close enough. "I went to find food," he explained. "I didn't know I'd come back to a full

87

house, or I would have brought more." When Raymond's eyes landed on Zoe, he tensed.

"Everyone, this is Zoe," Aldo jumped in. "Until yesterday, she belonged to Pam."

"But he left her behind in the—" Kate exclaimed, then quickly cut her sentence short. She looked at Aldo in a panic.

"In the fire," Aldo finished. Spencer knew that Marguerite, Darwin, Ro Ro, Kenny, and Raymond had probably been through a lot over the last day, but there was no sense in hiding the facts from them.

"He burned down Bearhaven, didn't he?" Raymond asked gravely.

"We guessed as much, from all the smoke. We could see it billowing from here," Marguerite explained.

"He did," Spencer answered. "And he left Zoe behind."

Zoe bent her head down, as if to show the other bears her bandages. "I got hurt, but Spencer, Aldo, and Kate saved me."

"We were even able to take out her microchip!" Kate gushed.

"So we can trust you?" Ro Ro asked.

"You can trust me," Zoe said. "As much as you trust my mother."

Ro Ro and Raymond exchanged a look.

"Zoe is Pinky's missing daughter," Spencer explained. His arms were still wrapped around Darwin, who was watching everyone else speak, his eyes wide.

Raymond looked Zoe over again, too, obviously shocked. "We thought you were dead," he said after a long moment.

"Pinky's been heartbroken all these years . . ." Marguerite whispered, her eyes locked on Zoe.

Zoe looked away.

"Such unfortunate timing . . ." Ro Ro gave Zoe a sympathetic look.

"Or maybe it's good timing!" Spencer exclaimed, desperate to change the darkening mood in the tree. "Zoe's going to help us stop Pam, and free the bears he's already captured. That's the plan at least."

"We're not giving up hope," Aldo said.

"We have to get Winnie back!" Kenny demanded.

"And Pinky." Raymond nodded at Zoe.

"And—" Kate started, but Spencer gently cut her off. This list could go on all day.

"We're going to get them all back," he said. "And, Darwin, we'll get your mom, too."

"Shhh!" Aldo's ears were twitching. Spencer looked around. The rest of the bears' ears were alert, their snouts moving rapidly. They were obviously hearing something, too. A second later, there was a hushed rumbling through the trees. Spencer held his breath. He knew that sound now. It was a pickup truck, rolling through the woods.

After a minute, the rumbling sound started to get quieter. The truck was moving farther away. They were safe for now, but it was obvious they couldn't wait in this tree any longer, hoping Pam's bear army wouldn't come back around. They were going to need somewhere safer to hide, and plan.

17

Spencer set out on his own to find a safer place to hide out. He knew exactly where he was going. He'd been there before. He just wasn't sure how welcome he'd be when he arrived.

When the small white house came into view, it looked just the same as the last time he'd been there. Its paint was still peeling, and its metal roof was still spotted with rust. Spencer glanced over at the dirt driveway as he stepped up onto the rickety front porch. It was empty. Just as Spencer had hoped, Kirby's mom wasn't home.

Beep, beep, beep. Spencer looked straight at the little surveillance camera perched above a nearby window and waved. By now, Kirby had seen him. He knew that anytime someone stepped up to the front door, the camera sent a picture of the porch and anyone standing on it to the computer in Kirby's bedroom.

The front door swung open. "You'd better make this quick. I'm very busy right now," Kirby announced, crossing her arms. "And don't expect to come inside. I don't trust you at all."

Spencer stepped back, surprised. "Uh . . . o-okay . . ."

he stammered, looking Kirby over. A paint-streaked green backpack was stuffed full and digging into her shoulders. She had three watches strapped to one wrist and a magnifying glass sticking out of one of her front pockets. An old, duct-taped-together Polaroid camera was hanging around Kirby's neck, and her curly hair was held away from her face by a camouflage-print bandanna. Aside from the bandanna, Kirby was dressed in all black.

"Well?" Kirby tapped her foot impatiently. "My surveillance has been going nuts, so I have to get out into the woods ASAP. I was just getting ready to go, and I don't have time to waste on *thieves* like you."

"Oh . . . right," Spencer said. It was obvious he was going to have to apologize to Kirby before he asked for her help again. She clearly hadn't forgiven him for the last time they'd been together, when Spencer had tricked Kirby and stolen her most prized finding from the woods— Kate's BEAR-COM. He'd done it to protect Bearhaven's technology from being discovered, but he still felt bad about it. After all, without Kirby's help, he, Aldo, and the Bear Council might never have figured out who had kidnapped Kate.

Spencer cleared his throat. "Kirby, I'm really sorry I messed with your equipment last time I was here, after you helped me and everything," he started. "But I had a really good reason. And I can make it up to you. I promise. Can I come inside? I can't explain it out here. It's not safe. But trust me, you want to hear this." Spencer saw Kirby hesitate. "I know you're mad that I stole the BEAR-COM—I mean, that thing I took from—"

"BEAR-COM?" Kirby asked, her curiosity getting the best of her. "That was a BEAR-COM? What's a BEAR-COM?"

"I'll tell you everything, if you let me inside." Spencer glanced over his shoulder. For all he knew, Pam, Margo, Ivan, and the guards were out patrolling this section of the woods right now. He couldn't say more until he was out of earshot, inside Kirby's house.

"Why should I trust you?" Kirby asked. "Maybe you'll just make up a bunch of stuff. It wouldn't be the first time, Mr. *Boy Scout*."

Spencer slipped off his backpack. He *had* lied about being a Boy Scout when he first met Kirby, but he knew there was one way he could definitely win her over. "You're right, I did lie," Spencer said, unzipping his backpack. "And I did take something from you. I'm really sorry, Kirby. Can I make it up to you? With a peace offering?" He dug around in the mission pack until he found his night-vision goggles. Kirby would never be able to resist spy gear. He pulled the goggles out. Kirby's eyes widened at the sight of them. "I'll give you these night-vision goggles if I can come inside and tell you what's going on."

Kirby looked away from the spy goggles as though trying really hard to resist Spencer's bargain. She shook her head. "I don't think so."

"Are you—" Spencer started, but Kirby's eyes immediately flicked back to the spy goggles and she cut him off.

"Fine! It's a deal!" She grabbed the goggles and stepped out of the doorway, giving Spencer room to pass. "Where did you even get these? They're so *nice*!" Kirby led the way to her bedroom, where Spencer knew she kept all of the high-tech gear she built from broken and cast-off computers, printers, cameras, and any other machines her security guard father sent her from California. Once they were inside the tiny room, Kirby sat down in her desk chair and spun around to face Spencer, the night-vision goggles still cradled in her hands.

"All right, I don't have much time, either," Spencer said. He didn't waste another second. "The reason you've seen so much suspicious bear activity in these woods is that a few miles from here, there's a hidden valley called Bearhaven, where until a couple of days ago, about a hundred bears were living."

"Impossible. I would have found it!" Kirby protested.

"You almost did a few times," Spencer explained. "But there's a really thick wall of trees surrounding it, and whenever you got too close, the bears could see you on their own surveillance. They'd use their security systems to keep you from getting any closer."

"The bears have . . . surveillance?" Kirby raised an eyebrow at Spencer suspiciously.

"Yes. They have all kinds of technology. And the most important piece is the BEAR-COM—that thing with pink sparkles on it that you found in the woods that I took back from you," Spencer hurried on. "It translates bear language, Ragayo, into English so they can speak to humans."

Kirby opened her mouth, as though to protest again, but Spencer cut her off.

"I can prove it," he said. "But listen, all the bears that lived in these woods, in Bearhaven, are rescued bears and their families. They've all either been freed from captivity where they were starving or treated really badly, or they've never been in the wild before because they were born in Bearhaven." Kirby nodded, and Spencer could tell she was starting to believe him now.

"The reason your surveillance has been going haywire is that Bearhaven's bears are in huge trouble," Spencer went on. "This horrible guy, Pam, wants to capture all of Bearhaven's bears and sell them for a bunch of money. Pam's an illegal bear trader, and he's been after Bearhaven for a long time." Spencer shook the thought of Pam's long clawlike fingernails out of his head. There wasn't time to get distracted. "Bearhaven's bears evacuated and were hiding in the woods, trying to escape to somewhere safe before Pam got here, but he ruined our plan and got here yesterday—a week earlier than we thought he could—and he ended up capturing almost everyone."

"How?" Kirby asked.

"He has an army of eighty-eight bears that he controls with microchip technology, and a bunch of guards with tranquilizer guns." Spencer sped on. "Bearhaven only has eight free bears left. But Pam won't leave until he gets them. Which is why—"

"How do you know all this? What do the bears have to do with you?" Kirby asked, suddenly suspicious again.

"My parents and my uncle Mark are the humans who helped start Bearhaven in the first place, and they're usually the ones who rescue the bears and bring them here. I've been here for a month. But, Kirby, we need your help—me and the eight free bears. Pam and his guards are out looking for us now. We need a safe place to hide and time to come up with a plan for how we can rescue the bears he's already captured, and I need to make a phone call to get us some backup." Spencer took a deep breath. "Can I bring them here?" he asked after a second. "You'll get to see how the BEAR-COMs work, and you can meet the bears. You can meet Kate! She's the cub you helped me save last time I was here. The one with the pink BEAR-COM."

"You want to bring eight talking bears to my house right now?" Kirby asked. "To hide from an evil bear trader, use my phone and my surveillance equipment, and come up with a plan to rescue a bunch *more* bears?"

Spencer hesitated, looking down at his sneakers . . . when Kirby put it that way, it did seem like he was asking a lot. "I guess so . . . yeah." He looked up at her hopefully.

"Well, why didn't you say so sooner!" Kirby exclaimed happily. "The more the bear-ier!" Kirby snorted out a laugh at her own joke. "Get it?"

18

Spencer stood guard on Kirby's front porch as one by one the eight bears emerged from the closest cluster of trees and bounded onto the porch and through the front door. Once all the bears were safely inside, Spencer stepped back into Kirby's house and closed the door behind him.

"I love it here!" Kate exclaimed, burrowing under the fluffy, candy-colored pillows covering the couch. Although Kate's BEAR-COM had been stripped down to be more discreet in the woods during Bearhaven's evacuation, the cub usually kept it studded with pink crystals. She loved pink sparkly things. And Kirby's mom, who worked in a craft store, obviously loved pink sparkly things, too, by the looks of the living room.

"Flowers inside?" Darwin asked as he wobbled onto his hind legs to sniff a bouquet of fake pink flowers. He buried his little snout in the dusty petals, then let out a huge sneeze and dropped back onto his butt.

"Kenny, that's not ours!" Ro Ro scolded. Spencer's attention snapped to the kitchen, where Kenny was practically climbing inside the open refrigerator. *Hopefully Kirby understood stuff like this might happen when she agreed to let us come here,* Spencer thought, looking around the house's tiny living room and kitchen. Bears seemed to be in every available space now, though the adult bears weren't quite as relaxed as the cubs.

Aldo stood beside Spencer, his back to the room as he peered out the window, keeping watch. Raymond had settled himself squarely in the middle of the kitchen and was staring at Kirby from there. Ro Ro kept glancing anxiously back and forth between Kenny, who was still rummaging through the fridge, and Kirby, who was standing in awed shock in the living room, her back against the wall. Zoe and Marguerite were squeezed in on either side of the plush couch with Kate.

"Thank you for having us," Marguerite said politely, her eyes on Kirby.

"I . . . you . . . I . . ." Kirby stammered as she stared back at Marguerite.

A clattering sound startled everyone.

"Sorry," Aldo muttered sheepishly. His claws were tangled in the window blinds' drawstring. "I thought we might want to cover the window, just in case." He tried to remove his claws from the string, and the blinds clattered again. Kirby rushed over.

"I can help you," she said, breaking her silence. "We should lock the door, too, even though I have very advanced technology to let us know if someone's out there."

"Right," Spencer agreed. He turned around and locked the door as Kirby tentatively reached for the string tangled around Aldo's claws.

"I won't make any sudden moves, I promise," Aldo said.

"Oh, I'm not worried about that," Kirby answered cheerfully. "I've been taking karate classes online, and my reflexes are really fast now. I bet I'd even be able to chop a block of wood in half with my hand." As Kirby chattered on, all the bears started to relax.

Spencer spotted a cordless telephone attached to the wall beside the fridge Kenny was still eyeing. He hurried over to it. The bears may be safer in here than out in the woods, but they still didn't have any time to waste. He grabbed the phone and turned back to Kirby, who was still explaining her karate lessons to Aldo as she lowered the blinds herself.

"Kirby, can I make a phone call?" he asked, interrupting her.

"Sure, go ahead," Kirby answered without turning

around. Spencer walked back to Kirby's bedroom, where it would be quieter, and sat down at her desk.

Spencer dialed Mom's cell phone number and lifted the phone to his ear. He took a deep breath. No matter how terrible things were, Spencer couldn't help but feel lucky that he could call Mom and Dad on the phone again. For weeks, he'd found himself in situations just as dangerous as this one, but Mom and Dad had been locked up by Pam and he'd had no chance to call and ask them for help.

"Hello?" Mom answered after one ring. Spencer was so relieved to hear her voice he couldn't even speak at first. "Hello?" she said again after a second.

"Mom, it's me," Spencer spoke up. A lump started to rise in his throat as he realized how bad the news he had to deliver to Mom and Dad was, and how badly he and the rest of Bearhaven's bears needed their help right now.

"Spencer! What's going on?" Mom asked right away, her voice all business. But before Spencer could answer, Mom had moved the phone away from her mouth. "Shane!" she called. "It's Spencer, come talk . . . I don't know yet . . ." Spencer heard a little shuffling around on the other end of the line, and then Mom was back. "Spencer, you're on speakerphone. Dad's here, too."

"What's going on?" Dad asked. Spencer could hear the fear in Dad's voice. "Are you hurt?"

"I'm not hurt," Spencer answered. "Where are you?"

"We're at the new Bearhaven," Mom replied quickly. "We were just getting ready to get on the road to come back. What's happened?"

"Pam is here," Spencer blurted out. "He got here early. Way early."

"How?" Mom demanded.

"Evarita just said—" Dad started, but Spencer cut him off as everything tumbled out at once.

"Evarita was captured. Pam has been using her to trick us. He got here yesterday with all these guards and trucks and the bear army and went straight to Bearhaven. He was furious there were no bears there, so he ordered his guards to set Bearhaven on fire and then he left. Aldo, Kate, and I were in the Lab, and we didn't know what was happening in the woods. We thought everyone who was hiding there would be okay overnight, but they weren't. Pam's guards tranquilized everyone. Only a couple of our bears got away. There are eight bears, and me. My friend

Kirby is hiding us. But I don't know what to do! I have Darwin, Kate, Aldo, Ro Ro, and Kenny with me, and Pam says he won't leave without Darwin or any of the bears he sold, which means his whole army is out searching for us right now. We have to stop him—"

"Whoa, whoa, whoa," Dad said. "Slow down, Spencer."

"How fast can you get here?" Spencer pressed on, his voice shaking. "We need to stop Pam and save all our bears."

"No," Mom said firmly, though her voice was full of emotion. "You need to take the bears you have with you and get out of there. It's too dangerous. Can you get to the TUBE station? From where you are?"

"Yes," Spencer said. "But—"

"All right, then get there," Mom ordered. "Who else is with you?"

"Raymond, Marguerite—"

"Perfect," Mom rushed on. "Have Marguerite take the TUBE to the last stop on the line and stay there. We'll come for you when we can, and you'll be safe until we do."

"But, Mom," Spencer answered, "we can't leave everyone Pam's already captured behind! What if Pam sends them back to Moon Farm?"

"We'll handle that," Dad answered. "We'll come with Uncle Mark and deal with Pam first. We'll do whatever we can to get the bears he has already captured back."

"When will you get here?" Spencer asked. This wasn't how he'd wanted this phone call to go.

"Tomorrow," Mom answered. "We're a day's drive away, but we'll come as quickly as we can."

"What if you're too late?!" Spencer practically shouted.

The other end of the line was quiet for a moment. Then Dad spoke up. "You, and the bears you have with you, will at least be safe. And we'll start working on rescuing everyone else—even if Pam moves them to Moon Farm—as soon as we can."

Spencer was about to argue again when a picture suddenly popped onto the computer screen on Kirby's desk in front of him. It showed Kirby's front porch, and the two people who had just stepped onto it.

"I have to go," he whispered into the phone, his eyes glued to the computer.

"What's wrong?" Mom asked immediately.

"I have to tell everyone the plan right away," Spencer answered, his stomach twisting guiltily as he lied. But there was no point telling them who was on Kirby's porch now. There was nothing Mom and Dad could do to help him. He'd said to his parents what he'd needed to: get here fast.

Knock, knock, knock.

"Bye," Spencer said loudly, over the sound of someone knocking on Kirby's front door, and hung up the phone. He launched himself out of the desk chair and crashed into Kirby, who was just racing into the room.

"Who are they?" Kirby asked frantically. She pointed to the picture on the computer screen that showed Margo and Ivan standing side by side on Kirby's front porch.

"Bad guys," Spencer said, his heart starting to beat faster and faster in his chest. "Really bad guys."

19

Spencer and Kirby scrambled to hide eight bears in Kirby's four-room house. Raymond, Marguerite, and Zoe crammed into Kirby's mom's bedroom. Kenny hid beneath Kirby's desk, which left just enough space in Kirby's bedroom for Ro Ro to jam herself inside. Kate and Darwin squeezed into the bathroom, with Darwin curled up in the sink and Kate's back two legs in the shower stall. And Aldo crouched out of view in the kitchen.

Knock, knock, knock!

"Hello? Anybody home?" Margo called from the porch. Spencer could tell she was trying to sound friendly, like a person casually stopping by in the middle of the day, but there was no hiding the raspy croak of her voice.

"Hurry!" Kirby whispered as Spencer dove behind the couch and immediately found himself covered in dust.

The house fell silent. Keeping Spencer and the free bears safe was up to Kirby now. Spencer heard the door open.

"Hello, who are you?" Kirby asked right away.

Margo coughed.

"I am Iv—" Ivan stopped speaking with a grunt.

Spencer guessed Margo had elbowed her brother to stop him from revealing their real identities.

"We are detectives," Margo said. "Looking into . . . something important that I'm afraid I can't tell you about." Spencer rolled his eyes from behind the couch. "You may be able to help us, young lady. Have you seen any bears lately?"

"Bears!" Kirby exclaimed. "I've been trying to see bears in these woods for ages! I see their tracks all over the place, you know. I mean, not near here but deeper into the woods," Kirby continued as Spencer realized with horror that there were probably bear tracks leading up to Kirby's front porch right now. *Why didn't I cover them?!* he thought, but was distracted by Kirby. "I *did* see a cub once a couple of weeks ago. Not the mother, though, which I thought was a little weird. Is that weird? Do you guys know a lot about bears?"

"Uh . . . yes. Well, some things," Margo answered, sounding confused. "Have you seen any cubs lately? As in today?" Margo pressed on.

"No way," Kirby said firmly. "In fact, I might not have even seen one a few weeks ago!"

"I'm sorry?" Margo asked.

"Oh, it's no problem," Kirby answered quickly, as though Margo had meant her words as a real apology. "Thanks for coming by!" Spencer heard the door start to swing shut, but then, with a thump, it stopped before closing all the way. "Excuse me, sir, your foot is in the way of my door." Spencer could hear the fear starting to bubble into Kirby's voice.

"I know," Ivan answered flatly.

"We're not quite finished here," Margo said. Spencer gulped. The edge had returned to Margo's voice. She wasn't pretending to be nice anymore.

"What else can I do for you?" Kirby asked, trying to sound cheerful.

"Could we have a look around?" Margo asked.

"I don't own the woods," Kirby answered. "Look all you want!"

"Around your home, perhaps?" Margo said, trying to get her voice to sound friendly-ish again.

"Oh, no, sorry," Kirby said right away. "My mom's been sick all day. Food poisoning. It smells pretty barfy in here. And she just went to bed. She's asleep. So I really can't let you in. But—"

Bringgggg!

Spencer nearly jumped out of his skin at the sound of the phone ringing.

Bringgggg!

"Should you answer that?" Margo asked.

"Oh." Kirby sounded as though she'd just realized the phone was ringing.

"Before your *mom* wakes up?" Spencer could imagine Margo raising one skinny eyebrow at Kirby right now.

Bringgggg!

"Yes, one second." Spencer heard footsteps run across the small room, then dart right back to the doorway.

"Hello?" Kirby said into the phone. Spencer gulped, sure it was Mom and Dad calling to figure out what was going on. "Oh, hi, Dad!" Kirby exclaimed as though it was her own father. "When will you be home? . . . Ten minutes? . . . Oh, five? Great! Did you pick up dinner? Mom's still sick . . . Uh-huh . . . What are we having? . . ." *Wrap it up, Kirby!* Spencer wanted to yell. "Is Big with you? . . . Cool . . . Okay, bye!" There was a beep as Kirby ended the phone call. "My dad's almost here. Maybe he can answer more of your questions. Or his friend Big," Kirby went on. "He's a security guard, just like my dad. We call him Big because he's a really huge guy. Like even bigger than you, Detective Iv."

There was a brief silence.

"Oh, that's all right," Margo said after a second. "I think we have all we need for now."

"Okay, bye!" Kirby said, and this time, when she swung the door shut, it closed all the way. Spencer wanted to cheer as he listened to her slide the lock into place.

20

"That was awesome!" Spencer crawled out from behind the couch and brushed the dust off himself.

"Good work, Kirby," Aldo added, stepping out of his hiding place in the kitchen and giving a big full body shake.

"That was *nuts*! I've never acted or done anything like that." Kirby rushed to the back of the house excitedly as she continued to talk. "They were so weird!" Kirby flung open the doors to the two bedrooms and the bathroom. "Those creeps are gone!" she announced triumphantly. "You can come out now."

"That was too close," Marguerite said as the bears emerged from their hiding places. Spencer sat down on the couch and put his head in his hands. He had to think. Seeing Marguerite had reminded him of Mom and Dad's specific orders: to leave the bears Pam had captured behind and take the TUBE as far from here as possible.

"What's wrong?" Kate asked quietly, startling him. Spencer looked up. Kate and Darwin had come to sit on either side of him, and everyone else was watching him with concern.

"Oh, I was just trying to figure out what to do next," he answered.

"What did Jane and Shane say?" Raymond asked.

"My parents are coming with my uncle Mark as fast as possible, but they won't be here until tomorrow," Spencer said. He tried to ignore the unhappy looks that the bears exchanged at the news that Mom and Dad couldn't get here immediately. "They want us to leave—"

"Leave!" Ro Ro exclaimed. "But what about the others?"

Spencer opened his mouth to answer but closed it right away. He didn't know what to say. He didn't want to leave the captured bears behind any more than anyone else here did, but he had specific instructions from Mom and Dad . . . Everyone kept watching him.

"Uncle B.D. and Uncle John Shirley will come with us?" Darwin asked, breaking the silence in the room. Spencer looked down at the cub, at a loss for words. His head was filled with the image of B.D. and John Shirley, tranquilized and piled in the back of a pickup truck.

"We have two choices," Spencer said, looking around the room. "We can leave now and almost guarantee that we'll all escape by taking the TUBE to the farthest stop, and wait there until my family can bring us to the new Bearhaven."

"And leave everyone else to Pam?" Zoe asked, though Spencer knew she was only thinking of Pinky.

"Yes," Spencer answered, then had to raise his voice to speak over all the grumbling that broke out in the room.

"But my parents and Uncle Mark would come here first and try to stop Pam and try to rescue the other bears."

"It's too big a risk," Aldo spoke up. "It's too long to leave Pam to his own devices. We wouldn't even know what he was doing. We would have no idea where he was going or where he might take our bears."

"What if he leaves for Moon Farm or takes them somewhere else?" Marguerite chimed in.

"They could be lost to us forever," Raymond added.

"Letting them get taken to Moon Farm sounds bad enough," Kate said quietly, pawing at her scarred ear.

"It's not what I want to do, either," Spencer said. "The second option—which goes against what my parents want us to do—is we stay, which is riskier for all of us but gives the captured bears a better chance of being rescued. We could try to find a way to stop Pam ourselves. Or at least delay him until my family is here."

"Is it even possible?" Ro Ro asked. "That bear army . . ." She glanced awkwardly over at Zoe.

"The bear army isn't as dangerous as it seems," Zoe said firmly.

"What do you mean?" Aldo asked.

"I mean, the way the attack command is programmed, the bears aren't supposed to injure the target," Zoe started to explain. "There are rumors that a higher level of attack exists, but we've never trained for it and it's never been used." Spencer glanced over at Kirby. He was sure she was bursting with questions, dying for someone to fill her in on everything, but she sat on the floor, her back propped up against her front door, watching the discussion in wide-eyed silence. "The bear army's job—what we train for—is just to scare the targets toward the guards," Zoe went on. "Or trap the targets long enough for the guards to come tranquilize them."

"It makes sense that Pam would only tranquilize us," Raymond said gravely. "Commanding the bear army or his guards to do any more harm would be too risky. If Pam wants to sell us, we can't be damaged goods."

Ro Ro shuddered and looked away. "I don't know what to do," she said sadly. "Risk the life of the one cub I have for the chance to save my daughter, or take Kenny to safety, and hope for the best for Winnie . . . Either way I'm risking one cub's life to save the other."

"You don't have to risk my life, Mom," Kenny piped up. "I can risk it myself. I'm staying."

Ro Ro started to protest, but Zoe interrupted her.

"I'm staying, too," she said. "I've belonged to Pam for as long as I can remember. I gave up hope of being rescued. I'll risk belonging to him again if it means I get to see my mom one more time."

"It could just as easily have been any of us Pam captured," Raymond said. "If it was us tranquilized on those trucks, I'd hope the free bears would stay and fight for me."

"They would," Marguerite said simply. "Just like I would stay for any of you."

"Kate?" Aldo asked from across the room.

"I don't think I'd ever be happy again if we didn't at least *try* to save our family," she said.

Aldo nodded, and Spencer could tell he was proud of his sister. "Well, I took an oath to protect Bearhaven and its bears," he said. "So I'm not going anywhere."

"I'll go where you go, Spencer?" Darwin asked.

"Yeah, Darwin," Spencer answered, and pulled the cub up onto the couch to sit beside him. "We're sticking together. All of us." He looked around the bear-crowded room. "So we're going to stay and do the best we can to stop Pam from leaving with any of the captive bears?" Everyone nodded back at him. *Now all we need is a plan . . .*

21

But there wasn't time to make a plan. Not at Kirby's house. Her mom was coming home from work soon, and Spencer and eight bears couldn't be there when she arrived.

"Here," Kirby said, pressing a walkie-talkie into Spencer's hand. He and the free bears were going to the TUBE for the night, to use the supplies there and decide their next move, but Kirby wasn't happy about having to stay behind. "Keep me updated. I can help you again tomorrow as soon as my mom leaves for work. You can use my equipment and stuff. Or I could come meet you! At the TUBE! Or wherever you are."

"Thanks, Kirby. I'll let you know." Spencer slipped the small walkie-talkie into his pocket. "We'd better get moving." He looked at the bears, who were lined up from just inside Kirby's front door, all the way to her bedroom. They were ready to make a break for the TUBE. Darwin was already holstered to Spencer's chest with a secure length of rope.

A chorus of "Thank you, Kirby" rang through the house as Spencer took his place at the front of the line, ready to open the door.

"I'm going on three," Spencer said loudly, so that everyone would hear him.

"And remember," Aldo called from the very back of the line, "if you get separated from the group, or if we run into any trouble, just get to the TUBE. We'll all meet there."

Spencer turned back to the door and reached for the knob. "One. Two. Three!" He flung the door open wide and crossed Kirby's front porch with one flying leap. He hit the ground and started to sprint down the short dirt path to the woods, holding Darwin tightly against him. He could hear the bears lumbering across the porch behind him, and within seconds, Marguerite, Raymond, and Zoe had passed him and were plunging ahead into the darkening woods.

"Spencer!" Kirby suddenly shouted over the sound of tires spinning on gravel. "It's them!" Spencer spun around. A pickup truck accelerated out of Kirby's driveway and across her front lawn, heading straight for Spencer. Spencer couldn't see past the blinding headlights into the truck, but he didn't have to. He knew it was Margo and Ivan.

"Everyone get to the woods!" Spencer cried. He wrapped his arms around Darwin, trying to hide the prized cub from view as he turned to continue his own sprint to safety. But he was too late: Margo had seen who he was carrying.

"Give me the cub or I shoot!" Margo's voice shrieked as the pickup truck pulled up beside Spencer. Margo was leaning out of the passenger-side window, a tranquilizer gun clutched in her arms and aimed straight at the fleeing bears.

What do I do?! Spencer started to panic. He was running as fast as he could, but he'd never be able to outrun a pickup truck! Up ahead, he saw Kate disappear into the woods. Aldo, Ro Ro, and Kenny were nearly there. Spencer wasn't going to make it. He turned back to Kirby's house, expecting the pickup truck to slam on its brakes and come after him.

"YOU HEARD ME, PLAIN!" Margo shouted.

Whoosh! Thump!

"No!" Spencer cried. He spun around. Kenny was lying on the ground at the tree line. Ro Ro was beside him, trying to drag the unconscious cub to safety. Aldo ran to help her, but the pickup truck was still heading straight for them. Suddenly, Kirby was beside Spencer. She had something clutched in her hands.

"Get her to turn back," Kirby hissed.

"What are you—"

"Just do it! Before she shoots again!" Kirby cried as she chased the truck. Spencer started after her just as Margo took aim at Aldo.

"FINE!" he yelled at the top of his lungs. "You can have him!" The truck slammed on its brakes. Margo turned back, an obnoxious smile on her face. She saw Kirby running straight for her, with Spencer just behind, and her smile faltered, but before she could react, Kirby lifted whatever was in her hand and sprayed something through the open car window into Margo's face. Margo started to howl in pain, her eyes squeezed shut, and Spencer saw his opportunity. He dodged around Kirby and knocked the tranquilizer gun out of Margo's hands. It fell to the ground.

"IVAN!" Margo shrieked, her eyes still closed as she frantically swiped at her face. "Do something! Get them!"

"Kirby, come on!" Spencer yelled. He grabbed the tranquilizer gun from the ground and sprinted for the woods. Aldo, Ro Ro, and Kenny were out of sight. He could hear Kirby just behind him, and then the sound of the pickup truck door opening.

"He's coming after us!" Kirby cried. Spencer looked over his shoulder. The hulking, freakishly strong Ivan was gaining on them.

"Just run!" Spencer called as the sounds of Ivan's heavy footsteps got louder.

"Spencer!" Kirby yelled.

"Ahhh!" Spencer was yanked off his feet. He dropped the tranquilizer gun to the ground. Ivan had him by the backpack.

"Leave him alone!" Kirby threw the spray can she'd been holding straight at Ivan, but it just hit his helmet and bounced off. Spencer twisted and kicked, trying to get away, but Ivan was carrying him backward toward the truck.

"Let me go!" Spencer yelled, finally spinning himself around in Ivan's grip to face his captor. He punched Ivan in the chest as hard as he could and winced at the pain of hitting the solid wall of muscles. With a grunt, Ivan released his grip, and Spencer, with Darwin secured at his chest, dropped roughly to his hands and knees on the ground.

That punch worked? Spencer thought, confused as to how his fists could actually slow Ivan down, until he heard thundering footsteps and felt two bears run up on either side of him. Spencer scrambled backward, then got to his feet.

Ro Ro and Aldo were huffing, grunting, and swatting viciously at Ivan. Ivan backed away slowly, until Aldo charged. Ivan turned and fled to the pickup truck, leaped into the driver's seat, and sped off before he'd even closed the door behind him.

"Kenny's tranquilized," Ro Ro said frantically. "We have to get him to the TUBE." With that, the mother bear turned and ran back into the woods.

"Kirby, do you have something that could help us move Kenny? Something with wheels?" Aldo asked, but before Kirby could answer, the sound of a car coming up the driveway silenced them all.

"My mom!" Kirby exclaimed. She grabbed the tranquilizer gun from the ground and headed back toward her house. "Spencer, come with me!"

Spencer hesitated, then decided that trusting Kirby's judgment had worked so far. He might as well keep it up.

"I'll meet you in the woods," Spencer called over his shoulder to Aldo as he ran to catch up with Kirby. They sprinted into Kirby's house, and she slammed the door shut after them. As they rushed back into Kirby's bedroom, Spencer heard the car stop in the driveway and turn off.

"She just parked!" he whispered, closing Kirby's bedroom door.

"That's okay," Kirby whispered back as she crouched down on the floor and started to rummage for something way under her desk. "Just get ready to go out the window."

Spencer climbed up onto the desk and quietly eased

the screen in the window behind it open. "Hey, Kirby," he whispered. "What was that stuff you sprayed at Margo?"

"Bear spray," Kirby answered with a grunt as she emerged from under the desk pulling something behind her. "Until today I had no idea that the bears around here were friendly. I always keep bear spray with me just in case I run into one in the woods. Ever since we saw that cub—I mean, Kate—a couple weeks ago."

"Kirby?" a woman's voice called. "I'm home."

"I'll be right out!" Kirby answered, and waved Spencer out the window. He jumped to the ground as quietly as he could, then turned back to find Kirby shoving a big black rolling suitcase out the window after him.

"Take this, for Kenny," she whispered once Spencer had grabbed the suitcase. "I've been keeping it in case my dad wants me to visit him in California. But I'll get it back from you later." Kirby closed the screen, then disappeared from view. Spencer could hear her bedroom door open. "Hi, Mom!" she called from somewhere Spencer couldn't see.

"I like Kirby," Darwin said, speaking up for the first time since Margo and Ivan's attack. Spencer guessed that fear had kept the cub silent.

"I like her, too, Darwin," Spencer answered. "She saved us tonight, that's for sure."

22

Using Kirby's rolling suitcase and a rope from Spencer's mission pack, Spencer, Aldo, Ro Ro, and Kate managed to get to the TUBE station with the tranquilized Kenny in tow.

"I'll get Marguerite!" Spencer said, jumping out of the tree elevator the second it opened to the TUBE platform. As the TUBE attendant, Marguerite was always prepared to help newly rescued bears if they arrived injured. She'd even helped Aldo after he'd been tranquilized in the last mission. "Marguerite!" he called, bursting onto the TUBE through one of its many open doors.

Spencer found Marguerite in the passenger car with Raymond and Zoe, who had the same awed look on her face as when she'd first seen the TUBE just this morning.

"What is it?" Marguerite asked, springing into action. "Is someone hurt?"

"Kenny," Spencer answered. "He's been tranquilized."

"Thank goodness he didn't get captured, too." Raymond rose from one of the big bear-sized passenger seats to follow Spencer and Marguerite.

"Tell them to bring him to the medical car," Marguerite said. "I'll get an antidote ready."

When Spencer and Raymond raced back to the TUBE platform Aldo and Ro Ro were only steps from the train. Kate was behind them, nudging the suitcase along with her snout. It was obvious that Ro Ro was exhausted from pulling the extra weight through the woods.

"Let me take your spot, Ro Ro," Raymond said gently, stepping up to the mother bear's side. Ro Ro nodded and dropped the rope she held in her mouth. "We're taking him to the medical car, Aldo." Raymond picked up the rope, and he and Aldo pulled Kenny farther down the train.

"Come on," Spencer said to Kate, heading back toward the passenger car. "Let's go check on Zoe. Kenny will be fine now."

"I'm hungry," Darwin said sleepily from his place in the harness at Spencer's chest.

"Me too," Kate answered as they all joined Zoe in the passenger car. Spencer sank gratefully into one of the bear-sized seats. It was just as comfortable as ever. He started to untie the rope binding himself and Darwin together.

"What happened?" Zoe asked as she tapped buttons on the side of her seat. "Whoa!" the seat tipped back, turning into a bed. She tapped the button again and returned to an upright position, then sheepishly turned her attention to Spencer and Kate, leaving the buttons alone.

"Margo and Ivan ambushed us." Spencer sighed. "They must not have believed Kirby after all."

Spencer woke up after a few hours and couldn't fall back to sleep. Once Marguerite had given Kenny a tranquilizer antidote, he'd woken up, and they'd all shared an anxious, exhausted meal in the dining car before deciding that what they needed more than anything else was sleep.

Now the passenger car was quiet, aside from the whistles and snores of eight sleeping bears, but Spencer's mind was racing. What if he'd made a huge mistake by not doing what Mom and Dad had told him to? Did he and the free bears even stand a chance against Pam and his army of bears and guards?

It's the tranquilizer guns we don't stand a chance against . . . he realized, thinking back to Margo and Ivan's attack in front of Kirby's house. If it hadn't been for Kirby's quick thinking—and her bear spray—Spencer wasn't sure Aldo or Ro Ro would have escaped being shot . . . If Pam's guards could knock bears out with a single shot, Spencer didn't see what he and eight free bears could do to stop Pam . . . unless they started by stopping the tranquilizer guns . . .

Spencer shifted in his seat, trying to get more comfortable, and something in his pocket jabbed him. He reached for it, and found the walkie-talkie Kirby had given him. Spencer pulled it out and looked it over, thinking back on what a good teammate Kirby had turned out to be today. She'd even thought to grab Margo's tranquilizer gun from the ground. Spencer guessed she did it so that her mom wouldn't discover the weapon, but it also meant that Margo and Ivan wouldn't be able to use it again.

Wait a minute . . . Kirby had a tranquilizer gun! Spencer looked back down at the walkie-talkie. He knew it was late to call. Really late . . . but maybe Kirby wouldn't mind . . . Spencer quietly lifted the cocoon hood of his seat, stood up, and silent-walked through the back of the passenger car and into the wardrobe car.

"Kirby?" he said quietly into the walkie-talkie once he was settled on the floor, leaning up against the wall of mirrors. A few long moments passed in silence. "Kirby?" he said again.

"Spencer?" Kirby's groggy voice crackled out of the walkie-talkie.

"Kirby!" Spencer exclaimed. "I'm sorry to wake you up. But I think I need your help. Again."

"Okay, I'm ready," Kirby answered, sounding wide awake and all business. "But if it's more suitcases you need, I can't help you. I only have that one."

"It's not suitcases. It's the tranquilizer guns. We have to disable them somehow but without the guards knowing about it," Spencer explained. "Can you get a dart out of Margo's tranquilizer gun?"

"Hold on, let me see."

Spencer sat in the dark wardrobe car, waiting for Kirby to respond. If they could somehow make the darts harmless, then he and the free bears might actually stand a chance!

"Got one," Kirby's voice crackled into the room again. "I had to shoot one of the couch pillows to get it! But I have it now."

"We have to figure out how to get the liquid out of it so that when the guards shoot, the bears don't get tranquilized," Spencer answered, deep in thought.

"Okay, I'll look it up on the Internet . . . How to remove tranquilizer from a loaded dart," Kirby said slowly, as though she was speaking aloud as she typed. "It would take a thousand years for us to get the tranquilizer out of all their darts," she said after a second. "We'd have to take them apart, one by one."

"We don't have a thousand years," Spencer muttered.

"Why don't we just steal the guns?" Kirby asked.

"We want the guards to *think* they can tranquilize the bears," Spencer explained. "If they discover the tranquilizer guns are missing completely, they'll come up with some other way of capturing our bears. And my guess is, whatever they'd come up with next, we wouldn't like any better than tranquilizer guns."

"Oh, that's smart!" Kirby sounded impressed. Spencer felt himself blush, and for a second, he was glad he was alone in the dark wardrobe car so nobody would see.

"Thanks . . . Can we—"

"We'll depressurize them!" Kirby exclaimed. "I'm watching a video on how to do it right now. It just takes a pin, and a second. When the darts are depressurized, they won't release what's inside."

"That's perfect! I can get the pins," Spencer immediately started to plan.

"I'll study this video to make sure I know what we have to do," Kirby answered.

"We'll have to get in and out before sunrise," Spencer said, checking his watch. "It's two a.m. now. Can you be ready to go in an hour?" Spencer asked, then realized what he was doing. He was planning a dangerous mission . . . with Kirby. "I mean, you don't have to—"

"I'll be ready," Kirby cut him off.

23

One hour later, at three a.m. Spencer was standing outside Kirby's bedroom window with a loaded mission pack on his back and the pins from two lock-picking kits in his pocket. He had woken up Kate to tell her where he was going, just so someone else knew where he was in case things went wrong. And although Spencer and Kirby's plan to sneak into Pam's camp had made Kate really nervous, she'd still promised to stay quiet and only update the rest of the bears on Spencer's whereabouts if they woke up before he returned.

"Right on time," Kirby whispered, appearing in the dark window. Spencer watched, through the set of night-vision goggles he'd found in the wardrobe car, as she quietly pushed the screen up and swung her legs out the window. She jumped to the ground with a clatter that made Spencer flinch. The beat-up old Polaroid camera was back around Kirby's neck, and she had a backpack on, too.

"What's the camera for?" Spencer whispered once they'd jogged far enough from Kirby's house that there was no chance of her mother hearing.

"Collecting evidence," Kirby answered. Spencer gulped.

Aside from her own scouting of the woods looking for bears, he knew Kirby had never been on a mission like this before. While he definitely needed her help, and he was glad she seemed to be in operative mode already, Spencer hoped her habit of "collecting evidence" wouldn't get in the way of the mission ahead.

Spencer slowed when the circle of trucks finally came into view. "There it is," he whispered, pointing up ahead. He ducked behind a tree and felt Kirby squeeze in beside him. They leaned out from opposite sides of the trunk to get a good look at Pam's camp.

The camp glowed green through the night-vision goggles, but Spencer didn't see any humans or bears moving around. It seemed like the coast was clear.

"We'll have to keep an eye out for guards," he whispered, ducking back behind the tree. "But let's go find where they keep the tranquilizer darts. They have to be stored in one of the big trucks. The trailer is Pam's special lair. He wouldn't let them store supplies in there."

"Where are all the bears?" Kirby asked.

"Locked in cages on four of the big trucks," Spencer answered. "Two of the trucks have Pam's army in them, and two of the trucks have Bearhaven's captive bears. But there's a fifth truck. It must be supplies. I'm just not sure which are the four trucks filled with bears and which one is for the supplies."

Spencer set his mission pack on the ground and pulled out one of the latest additions to his bag. This one hadn't come from the wardrobe car; he'd found the bear-sized stethoscope in the medical car on his way out. He'd had a feeling it would be useful. Now he knew why. Spencer slung it around his neck like a doctor.

"Follow me." Spencer crept out from behind the tree and silent-walked the distance to the closest truck. He stayed hidden by as many trees as possible on his way there. Kirby followed along behind him, and with every step, she got a little quieter, as though she were studying Spencer's movements and learning from them as she went. When they reached the truck, Spencer made sure they stayed behind one of the truck's wheels, just in case there was a guard in the middle of the camp, keeping an eye on the surroundings. He crouched low to the ground, and out of the corner of his eye, he saw Kirby do the same.

"Do you see anyone?" she whispered as they searched the center of the camp for guards. Spencer shook his head, not wanting to risk saying anything out loud. He saw a cluster of tents. *The guards must all be asleep in those,* he thought, and stood back up, ready to start the search for the tranquilizer darts. He took the stethoscope from around his neck and tried to fit the earpieces into his own ears. They were too big, so instead, he held them against his ears as best as he could, then took the round silver head of the stethoscope and pressed it up against the truck's outer wall.

He jerked the stethoscope away from the truck, surprised by how loudly he could hear the sounds of bears shifting and grunting inside. After a second, he put the stethoscope back to take another listen.

"There are bears in this one," he whispered to Kirby once he was positive his ears weren't playing tricks on him.

He handed over the stethoscope. Kirby did the same thing he had. After she'd pressed the stethoscope to the truck, her eyes widened, and she nodded excitedly.

"Come on." Spencer waved her toward the next truck. They crossed the space between the two trucks carefully, but there still wasn't any sign of guards.

"Bears," Kirby whispered once she'd listened to the next truck. She passed the stethoscope back to Spencer and they took off for the next truck.

When Spencer pressed the stethoscope to the third truck, he didn't hear anything. No sounds of bears or movement. *Finally!* he thought. He quickly shoved the stethoscope back into his mission pack. "This is the one," he whispered. He and Kirby crept to the truck's back

doors. To Spencer's relief, they were unlocked. "Keep an eye out," he said. Kirby nodded back, her eyes glued to the center of camp.

Spencer quietly unlatched the back doors and eased one open just enough for himself and Kirby to slip inside. He climbed up into the truck, expecting Kirby to follow.

Click! Buzzzz . . .

Spencer froze at the shockingly loud sound and then spun around. Kirby was still just outside the door, a Polaroid picture clutched in one hand. Spencer reached out and grabbed her by the arm. She scrambled up into the truck, and Spencer closed the door behind her just as the sounds of tents unzipping filled the pitch-black night.

24

Spencer felt like his whole body was being crushed by bear kibble. He'd only just managed to wedge himself between two enormous bags of the bear food before the doors to the supply truck had swung open. Now the wide beam of a flashlight was bobbing around the cavernous space, searching for intruders.

Please be hidden, Kirby. Please, please be hidden, he thought to himself as he waited for the guards to spot him or Kirby and lunge into the truck to capture them.

Instead, after a few agonizing moments, a deep voice called out, "This one's clear," and the doors swung shut again.

Spencer took a deep breath as he listened to the sounds of guards shouting back and forth to one another around the camp. The truck they were in had been cleared. For now, he and Kirby were safe. He squeezed out of his hiding spot as quietly as he could.

"Kirby?" he whispered, scanning the supply truck. It was huge. Big wooden crates were stacked in the middle of the truck and shelves lined the sides. Spencer spotted trays upon trays of tranquilizer darts, but he didn't see Kirby anywhere. Then he heard shuffling behind him and spun around. Kirby climbed out of the wooden crate on the top of a stack, then carefully scaled two other crates to reach the floor again.

"I am *so* sorry," she whispered as soon as she was out of her hiding spot. "I didn't realize my camera was so loud! I never would have tried to take a picture if I'd known it would wake up the guards! It won't happen again, I promise."

"It's okay," Spencer answered. "We got really lucky they didn't find us." There was no sense in spending any more time on Kirby's loud mistake. "Let's just get to work." He strode over to the shelves stacked high with trays of tranquilizer darts. It seemed like there were thousands of them. "This could take a while," he muttered.

"Not once we get the hang of it," Kirby said, coming to stand beside Spencer. She reached out and gingerly pulled a dart from its place in the tray. "I practiced at home. It only takes a second."

"Here." Spencer dug the lock-picking kit pins from his pocket. He handed one to Kirby.

"Okay, watch this," Kirby said. "See this cap?" She pointed to a little plastic cap that covered the flat end of the dart, then plucked it out of position and folded it carefully in her palm. "First you have to take that out. Then you take your pin and stick it in the dart until you hit something," Kirby spoke slowly as she inserted the pin into the dart. "The thing you're hitting is a valve, and you want to push it forward until you hear a little whoosh sound. That's the dart depressurizing!"

Whoosh . . .

Spencer was pretty sure he only heard the sound because he was listening for it, but it was good enough for him.

"That's it!" Kirby whispered. "Then you just pull your pin out, put the cap back in, and you're done!" Kirby replaced her first dart in its tray. The dart looked exactly the same as it had before. No one would be suspicious that it had been deactivated. "Now you try."

Spencer carefully pulled a dart from the tray, his fingers shaking a little. He knew how dangerous the darts could be, and just the sight of it in his hand made him uncomfortable. He pulled off the dart's cap, then used his pin to repeat the motions he'd seen Kirby make.

Whoosh . . . Spencer smiled and replaced the depressurized dart's cap, confident for the first time that this dart plan would work.

"That's all there is to it," Kirby said, then looked at all the tranquilizer darts in front of them. "Times about a thousand."

Spencer replaced the newly disabled dart in its tray. "All right, I'll do half and you do half," he said. There were at least five shelves filled with empty trays, and Spencer's stomach twisted at the sight of them, knowing that meant that the hundreds of darts that used to be in those trays had already been fired at Bearhaven's bears. There were eight shelves left. "You take those four shelves," he said, pointing out Kirby's half. "And I'll take these four."

"I'll race you," Kirby said, grabbing the first dart in her first tray. "Winner gets to take a souvenir from in here." She waved her dart around the dark cargo space. "Deal?"

"Deal," Spencer answered, getting to work. *Kirby probably already has her eye on something she can take apart and add to her surveillance gear,* he thought. Not that he minded. The faster they both worked the better.

By the tenth dart, Spencer was so used to the motions that it took to depressurize them that he could pick up a dart, depressurize it, and return it to its place in the tray in under ten seconds. Out of the corner of his eye, he could tell Kirby was moving just as quickly.

"Done!" Kirby exclaimed in an excited whisper just as Spencer pressed the pin into his final dart. "In an hour flat! It's four-thirty now!"

"You win," Spencer said, replacing his dart. He was just happy they were done. He didn't mind that Kirby had beaten him to the finish. His fingers were cramping, and he felt like they'd been in the dark truck for hours. He was glad it hadn't really taken too long.

Kirby raced back to where she'd been hiding and grabbed something off a nearby shelf, then hurried to cram it into her already stuffed backpack. Spencer turned and headed for the back doors of the truck. *I'll have to find out what she took later,* he thought pressing his ear up against one of the doors to listen.

"Hear anything?" Kirby whispered, joining him.

"No," Spencer whispered back. "The guards must have all gone back to bed." Slowly, so that he wouldn't make a sound, Spencer opened the door just enough for himself and Kirby to slip through the crack.

Spencer stepped to the ground with a soft crunch. Kirby

did her best to step down quietly, too, but the sound of her feet hitting the ground made Spencer tense. Luckily, it was still pitch-black in Pam's camp. They had at least an hour before the sun started to rise. If it wasn't for the night-vision goggles, he wouldn't be able to see a thing, so he hoped the guards, if any of them were still awake, wouldn't be able to, either. Spencer scanned the camp. He didn't see anyone through the eerie green tint of his goggles, but still . . . something didn't seem right.

"Spencer," Kirby whispered. "The tents are empty."

"And the pickup trucks are gone," Spencer whispered back. "Pam's Hummer is, too." He looked to the cluster of tents, their flaps were unzipped. Kirby was right. They were empty.

The camp is abandoned . . . Spencer realized. *But why?*

25

Spencer crept up to the side of Pam's trailer. He and Kirby had done a full lap around the camp, searching for guards, or Margo and Ivan, but so far they hadn't seen a single human. Whatever had made everyone suddenly leave the camp unguarded in the middle of the night must have been serious, but Spencer decided he wouldn't worry about that now. He wanted to take advantage of the empty camp, and the cover of darkness, to free Bearhaven's captive bears, but he had to be sure Pam wasn't going to catch him in the act.

"You'll have to look," Spencer whispered. The window on the side of Pam's trailer was covered in a row of metal bars and was too high for him or Kirby to see into, but Spencer was determined to know if Pam was inside. Spencer dropped to all fours on the ground. "Climb on," he whispered.

"Spencer?"

"Hurry, Kirby. Step onto my back," Spencer urged. Now wasn't the time for a discussion.

"That wasn't me," Kirby answered.

Spencer looked up at Kirby. She was pointing to the

133

window. "Somebody in there knows you're here!" she whispered urgently. "Should we run for it?"

"No! Don't go!" the voice whispered before Spencer could answer.

"It's Evarita!" Spencer only barely resisted cheering.

"Who's—" Kirby started, but Spencer cut her off.

"She's on our side! She can help us! Pam must be gone, too!"

"He is," Evarita's voice confirmed. "But, Spencer—"

"Come on, Kirby!" Spencer called, not bothering to whisper this time as he scrambled to his feet and headed for the door to Pam's trailer. He threw the door open and ran inside. Pam's trailer looked like a miniature, fur-covered palace. A shiny black desk stretched along one side, with stacks of papers piled neatly across its top edge, each topped with a golden bear claw paperweight. Kirby raced inside after Spencer and then gasped as the door swung shut behind her. Spencer didn't have to turn around to know what had startled her. Pam's horrible throne sat in front of the desk. It was the number one most horrible piece of furniture Spencer had ever seen in his life, because it was made up of bear parts—fur, claws, even teeth. But disgusting as it was, he couldn't worry about the throne now.

"Spencer!" Evarita cried, snapping Spencer's attention to the caged-off section of the trailer. Evarita was there, her hands on the bars. Her knuckles were white from gripping the metal so hard.

"Evarita!" Spencer ran the short distance across the fur-covered floor to her.

"I'm so glad you're all right!" she said, her eyes locked

on Spencer. Evarita's long, wavy hair was pulled back into a ponytail. She looked stressed and exhausted.

"But you shouldn't be in here. It's too risky. Pam's furious. He discovered that Dora went missing an hour and a half ago. He thinks the Plains kidnapped her."

"The Plains?" Kirby asked.

"My parents," Spencer answered quickly. "That's why everyone's gone?"

"Dora took two other bears with her," Evarita hurried on. "Pam and Margo and Ivan and all the guards are out searching for them now. But you have to get out of here. He could be back any minute. I just wanted to tell you to find Dora. She's ready to help. To join our side."

"We'll get you out first!" Spencer exclaimed eying the padlock on Evarita's cage door. "Then you can—"

"No, Spencer," Evarita cut him off right away. "There isn't time!"

"But how do you—" Spencer started to protest, but the sound of a vehicle approaching cut him off. Spencer and Kirby froze.

The vehicle slammed on its brakes. The sounds of doors opening and slamming shut made Evarita jump.

"—and we'll tighten security," Margo's voice whined from somewhere much too close by. *They must have parked the Hummer right next to Pam's trailer!* Spencer realized as his heart started to hammer in his chest.

"Now what?!" Kirby mouthed to Spencer.

"Go out through the bedroom window!" Evarita hissed, frantically waving them toward a short, mirrored hallway.

"We'll leave every truck guarded all day and night," Margo continued, as though she was trying to plead for forgiveness and solve a problem at the same time.

"It's too late for that!" Pam yelled. His high-pitched voice was getting closer. "You should have had them guarded from the beginning!"

Spencer turned and sprinted on tiptoes to Pam's bedroom, waving for Kirby to follow. He leaped up onto the black-velvet-covered bed that took up half the room and nearly lost his balance on the plush surface. Kirby jumped up after him, and they both stumbled toward the window above the bed.

"They took three of our bears right out from under our noses," Pam's muffled voice continued angrily. "And Dora! Of all the bears! They took Dora!"

Spencer grasped for the screen in the window and slowly slid it out of place, his fingers shaking. He waved Kirby forward. She rushed in front of Spencer and climbed up into the window. A second later, she pushed herself off the windowsill and landed with a thud on the ground. Spencer held his breath, afraid the sound would give them away. Luckily, Pam was still yelling.

"I can't risk it happening again. I will not lose any more bears. I don't care how tight you tell me the security is going to be!"

Spencer climbed up into the open window. Kirby was a few feet away, pressed up against the side of the trailer. Spencer waited for Pam to start shrieking again. But now Pam's voice had dropped to a low sinister growl.

"We'll send the bears we have to Moon Farm tomorrow," Pam announced. "Fill one truck and get them out of here. There won't be much the Plains can do about it then."

No! Spencer sat frozen in place. Pam couldn't send a truckload of Bearhaven's bears to Moon Farm! Spencer and the free bears would lose their chance to rescue them!

"That's all! I'm going to bed!" The trailer door squeaked open.

"Spencer, come on!" Kirby whispered urgently.

"Hey!" Pam cried just as Spencer pushed off the windowsill and tumbled to the ground.

"What was that?!" Margo yelled from outside the trailer's front door.

"IVAN!" Pam shrieked.

Spencer felt Kirby grab onto his arm and pull him to his feet. He recovered his balance just as the sounds of heavy footsteps started to thunder around the side of the trailer toward him and Kirby.

"Run!" he whispered.

26

The sun was just starting to rise as Spencer and Kirby tore through the woods away from Pam's camp. The Hummer was after them, with Margo behind the wheel. Her greenish-blond hair flew crazily around her face as she steered the huge vehicle down the path through the woods at top speed.

Spencer dodged to the left, leaving the path to sprint into a denser part of the woods where the Hummer wouldn't be able to follow, and Kirby stayed close behind him. Her Polaroid camera and whatever gear she'd packed into her backpack clattered and jangled as she ran.

"Watch out!" Kirby suddenly shouted. The Hummer was speeding off, probably trying to find another way to follow Spencer and Kirby, but now a pickup truck was heading straight for them. Spencer had forgotten that all of Pam's guards were out in the woods now, searching for the three missing bears.

"This way!" Spencer veered off to the right, running even faster.

Beeeep! Beeeep! The pickup truck honked and hit the gas. Pebbles spewed out from under its wheels as the truck fishtailed then accelerated after Spencer and Kirby.

"They're gaining on us!" Kirby cried.

What are we going to do? Spencer started to panic. The Hummer had reappeared up ahead, cutting off their path. Spencer spotted a small clump of trees to their left. He didn't dare look back to see how close the pickup truck was now.

"Follow me!" he yelled to Kirby, then ducked into the trees at a sprint. A moment later, a jet-black bear paw plunged through the air toward him, reaching down from a nearby tree. He sprinted straight at it, then took a running leap and grabbed for the bear's leg, allowing himself to be scooped up into the branches of the tree.

"Ahh!" Kirby gasped from the ground.

Spencer grabbed for the tree trunk, getting a firm hold of it as the bear pulled away from him. He looked down. Kirby was frozen in place beneath the tree. Dora leaned out of the tree for her. Kirby hesitated, searching the branches for Spencer.

"Come on! You can trust her!" Spencer whispered urgently as soon as their eyes met. He heard the pickup truck slam on its brakes not far away. Then the sounds of truck doors opening and closing. A second later, Kirby was scooped up by a huge bear paw and deposited into the tree beside Spencer, and shouts were ringing through the woods.

"Hey! Kids!"

"Do you see them?!"

"They went this way! Come on!"

As the guards ran past, heading deeper into the trees, Spencer was careful not to move a muscle. He and Kirby were both breathing hard, but they didn't give themselves away. Dora was crouched on a branch just below them, watching the ground, ready to attack if the guards discovered them.

Ouch! Kirby elbowed Spencer. She pointed upward, and Spencer followed her gaze. B.D. and John Shirley were both perched in the branches above him. Just as Spencer had suspected, the two bears Dora had taken with her when she left Pam's camp were her two brothers.

Spencer had never seen the three Benally siblings—Dora, B.D., and John Shirley—together at the same time. Now he understood why Mom, Dad, and Uncle Mark had been so determined to set these three bears free all those years ago at Gutler University. The Benally siblings were each powerful-looking bears. It was obvious that they were never meant to be owned—and abused—by humans.

Spencer started to relax, just a little. With Dora, John Shirley, and B.D. free from Pam and on the side of Bearhaven's free bears, they might still have a shot at stopping Pam.

Pam's guards interrupted Spencer's thoughts.

"You lost them!" one shouted.

"*You* lost them! You shoulda driven faster!"

The guards were trudging back under the tree, heading for their pickup truck. "Pam's gonna kill us."

"Pam? We have to survive Margo first. And it's not gonna help any that we used almost all our tranquilizer darts out here tonight and don't have a single *bear* to show for it."

"We've got hundreds of darts back at the camp. I bet the others shot all their darts, too. It's not just gonna be us who needs another batch. Everyone will need to reload."

"Why are we chasing kids anyway?" one of the guards grumbled as the group moved farther away. Spencer listened to the sounds of the guards piling back into their truck, but he didn't hear an answer. The truck pulled away.

"We did it," he said to Kirby. The mission to disable the tranquilizer darts felt like it had begun days ago, but now it was officially over. They'd gotten out.

"Not alone," Kirby whispered, looking around the tree at the three full-sized bears. All three of them blinked back at her.

27

"I'm home," Kirby's voice crackled out of the walkie-talkie in Spencer's pocket. "And my mom's still asleep. Tell me the minute you make a plan! Good night! Or . . . good morning, I guess, is more like it." Kirby's laugh turned into a snort, and a second later, the walkie-talkie fell silent.

Spencer smiled. He was glad Kirby's mom hadn't woken up and discovered her missing. He and the free bears were probably going to need her help again today.

"*Ko?*" B.D. grunted the bears' word for "now." He, Dora, and John Shirley were standing in the tree elevator on the border of Bearhaven, waiting for Spencer to step inside so they could all lower into the TUBE station.

"*Ko,*" Spencer replied, squeezing into the wide, hollowed-out tree trunk with the bears and pressing the button to shut the doors. Without BEAR-COMs, any real discussion had to wait. Spencer had only barely managed to express that they needed to go to the TUBE using the little Ragayo he knew, and various hand motions.

The TUBE platform was abandoned, but the second Spencer stepped out of the elevator, Kate bounded out of the passenger car. Darwin was on her heels, tripping over his paws, his eyes wide, his nose and ears twitching.

"They smelled us," Spencer said, though he knew B.D., John Shirley, and Dora wouldn't understand his words.

"You've been gone for so long!" Kate cried, sliding to a stop in front of Spencer. "Everyone's awake! Aldo's mad you went on a mission without him!"

Aldo stepped out onto the TUBE platform. The rest of the free bears followed.

"I'm not mad," Aldo mumbled, though his eyes were focused on something over Spencer's shoulder. Spencer turned around. Darwin was jumping and flopping around Dora, trying to nip at her ears.

"Mom! Mom! Mom! You're here!" the cub sputtered, headbutting Dora and pawing at her frantically. Dora nuzzled the cub, and B.D. and John Shirley hovered close by, watching Darwin affectionately. "Don't go away again, Mom, okay? Okay, Mom?"

Spencer turned back to the free bears standing just outside the TUBE. He expected them to look happy, touched by the reunion, but he was surprised to find that everyone from Kate to Raymond looked pained. *They must be thinking about their own families . . . and whether they'll ever see them again,* Spencer thought. Suddenly, the fact that they needed a plan to stop Pam from sending a full truck of Bearhaven bears to Moon Farm *today* popped back into Spencer's head.

"Marguerite," he said, springing into action. "Are there extra BEAR-COMs on the TUBE?"

"Of course," Marguerite answered. She glanced over Spencer's shoulder at Dora, B.D., and John Shirley, then turned back toward the TUBE. "I'll get three," she called.

"What happened out there, Spencer?" Aldo asked.

"Yeah," Kate chimed in. "How'd it go?"

Spencer took a deep breath. The bears were staring at him expectantly. "Kirby and I disabled their whole supply of tranquilizer darts," he said, wanting to give them good news first. Everyone seemed to relax.

"Oh, thank goodness," Ro Ro gasped.

Spencer hesitated. "Once Marguerite gets those BEAR-COMs, and the Benallys are finished with their reunion, I'll tell you the rest," he said after a second. Spencer avoided Aldo and Kate's eyes, afraid they'd be able to tell that "the rest" wasn't such good news as he slipped past the bears to board the TUBE. His stomach growled loudly. Spencer knew that operatives' favorite foods were kept on the train for after missions, which meant that somewhere around here, he should be able to find himself some peanut butter toast.

"I didn't think they would discover we were gone until this morning," Dora went on. Everyone was gathered in the dining car, listening to Dora tell her side of the story of last night. Darwin sat wedged in beside Dora, as though determined to stay attached to her from now on. "But something must have given us away—"

"We did," Spencer cut in. "Kirby and I were there. She made a sound that woke up the guards, and then they searched all the trucks . . . I'm sorry," Spencer rushed on. "But your escape helped—"

"Why were you there?" B.D. asked gruffly. He shot Aldo a look as though to say, "Why was he there without your protection?"

"I realized that the tranquilizer darts were the biggest threat to us," Spencer motioned around the room, indicating everyone there. "So Kirby and I went to disable Pam's supply. I would have brought Aldo," Spencer said, glancing apologetically at the bear who had become his constant teammate. "But I was afraid to risk any of the few bears who are still free, and we only needed human hands in order to disable the darts anyway."

"And it worked?" John Shirley asked.

"Yes," Spencer answered. "They still have hundreds of darts, but now the darts won't release any tranquilizer when they're shot."

"I see," B.D. said, sounding impressed.

"And the guards have no idea that anything's changed with their darts?" Raymond asked.

"No, there's no way—" Spencer started.

"I have a question," Zoe interrupted him. There was an edge in her voice.

"Yes, Zoe?" B.D. said, staring her down. Spencer looked back and forth between Zoe and B.D. He was almost certain nobody had told B.D. who Zoe was.

"How do you know my name?" Zoe asked, sounding taken aback.

"I'm the Head of the Bear Guard. It's my job to know," B.D. answered gruffly. "And I once led a mission to rescue you," he went on, softening a little. "Your question?"

Zoe hesitated, but after a second, she looked to Dora. "Why did you only free *your* family?"

"I plan to help you free every one of the captive bears," Dora said, looking around the dining car as though she really wanted everyone to listen to her now. "And I know my brothers will, too. But without a plan or a place to take them, freeing any more bears than I did last night would have only put everyone in more danger. I chose to free B.D. because I know he has been the head of Bearhaven's security for years and has experience leading rescue missions. And John Shirley—" Dora looked back and forth between her brothers before going on. "I've been the sibling left behind before. I wasn't going to do that last night."

Before anyone else could speak up, Spencer cut in. "I know there's a lot to talk about," he started. "But we don't have time now. Pam thinks my parents rescued two bears from the trucks last night and kidnapped you, Dora. He still has no idea you're working with us. He's planning to send the bears he's already captured to Moon Farm sometime today—" Protests and questions erupted from all the bears around Spencer. He spoke louder. "He doesn't want to risk losing any more of the bears he's already got!" The noise in the dining car got louder still as the bears reacted to the news that their families were going to be sent to Pam's bear trafficking headquarters in a matter of hours. "WE HAVE TO STOP HIM!" Spencer shouted. "AND WE HAVE TO DO IT NOW!"

The dining car fell silent. Everyone stared at Spencer. After a moment, B.D. spoke up.

"Let's get to work," he said, taking charge.

28

Spencer stepped onto the TUBE platform. Behind him, he could hear the bears moving around the train quickly, making their final preparations for the mission ahead. For the first time in what felt like hours, he had a moment to think. He reached into his pocket and pulled out his jade bear.

"When will your parents be here?" Kate asked, trotting over to him. Kate knew all about Spencer's jade bear, and catching him looking at it now, she must have known he was thinking about Mom and Dad.

"They said today," Spencer answered. "Soon I hope." Spencer slid the figurine back into his pocket. Mom and Dad and Uncle Mark were coming as quickly as possible, but Spencer was here now. And he was going to make sure Bearhaven's captive bears were free again. "Are you ready?" he asked Kate.

"You bet I am!" the cub answered. "I'm going to run even faster than I ran from the bear army the first time!"

"And this time you'll have a head start!"

"Any word from Kirby?" Aldo asked. He and B.D. were just stepping out of the TUBE.

"Not yet. I'll radio her," Spencer answered. When Spencer had told Kirby the plan, she'd sprung into action. Now she was in the woods surrounding Pam's camp, installing boom boxes, speakers, and stereos from her collection of ragtag electronics. "Kirby, how's it going?"

Kirby's voice crackled excitedly through the walkie-talkie. "Mission accomplished! My loudspeaker work here is done!"

"Perfect!" Spencer radioed back. "We'll meet you in half an hour."

"Copy that. Over and out," Kirby replied, and Spencer slipped the walkie-talkie back into his pocket.

"Let's prepare to move," B.D. said. "Aldo, tell everyone to assemble here, on the platform." Aldo turned and trotted back on the TUBE. Not a minute later, the free bears were gathered around B.D., watching him expectantly. Spencer could feel the excitement rising in the TUBE station.

B.D. sat back on his haunches and surveyed the group. "You are all very brave to volunteer for this rescue mission," he started. "And you are all very important to its outcome. Each and every one of us must stay focused and stick to the plan for this to work." The bears nodded their understanding.

"Um, Spencer?" Kirby's voice broke in, interrupting B.D.'s mission send-off. Spencer grabbed the walkie-talkie out of his pocket.

"Yeah?" he whispered back to Kirby, though he knew everyone on the TUBE platform was watching him now.

"I'm at the meeting spot," Kirby said. "And I can see

into the camp from here. And the guards are unloading a bunch of bears."

Unloading the bears? The free bears exchanged confused and worried looks.

"Ask if the bears he's unloading are chained up," Aldo said right away.

"Kirby, are they chained up?" Spencer asked.

"No."

"The bear army," B.D. said grimly. "Not our bears."

"Pam must be sending them to hunt for us again," Dora said her eyes on B.D.

"But if he sends them out before we start our rescue mission . . . the plan won't work!" Kate exclaimed.

Kate's right, Spencer thought. The safety of their team of eleven free bears during the rescue mission depended on controlling where Pam's bear army went so that they would always know the bear army's location. If the bear army set out into the woods now, at Pam's orders, the free bears would lose the control they needed and—

"Tell her we're coming, Spencer," B.D. ordered, interrupting Spencer's thoughts. "We're leaving now."

With that, the Head of the Guard turned and crossed the distance to the elevator in a few fast paces. Spencer watched the rest of the free bears hurry after B.D., but he stood frozen in place. They hadn't finished the official mission send-off! They hadn't said *abragan*, the phrase that meant "for the bears," and was always said by everyone in unison right before a rescue mission. He'd started to think of the *abragan* chant as a good-luck tradition . . . but B.D.

was already stepping into the elevator. The moment had passed. Spencer gulped and lifted the walkie-talkie to his mouth.

"We're coming," he told Kirby, trying to ignore the sinking feeling he suddenly had about this mission. "We're coming now."

29

"Everyone's in position," Aldo reported as he climbed up into the tree where Spencer, B.D., Dora, Darwin, and Kirby were hiding. Spencer didn't take his eyes off Pam's camp, a short distance away. The bear army was lined up in rows, standing completely still while the guards loaded the pickup trucks with trays of the now-deactivated tranquilizer darts.

"Time for the bear sounds?" Kirby asked, looking around the tree. She was perched in the crook of a branch, an array of equipment in her lap and two remotes duct-taped to each other clutched in each of her hands.

"Yes, bear sounds now," B.D. answered, giving the order.

Kirby tapped a few buttons on the double remote, then spun a little knob. She paused, listening.

The loud bawling sounds of a cub in distress rose out of the woods somewhere in the distance.

Yes! It sounded just like a real bear! Spencer wanted to high-five Kirby, but she was busy cuing the five other stereos she'd installed in a ring around Pam's camp to start playing recorded bear sounds and set the plan in motion.

Truck engines roared to life, calling Spencer's attention back to Pam's camp as it erupted in chaos. Guards were running every which way, shouting and pointing in all different directions. Margo was barking orders, waving Ivan into the passenger's seat of a pickup truck as she headed for the driver's seat.

"It's coming from over there!"

"No, it's over there now!"

"There's more than one!"

"Split up! Go after all of them!"

"Don't come back here without bears!" Pam hollered through a golden megaphone, drowning everyone else out. He was standing in the door of his trailer, watching the mayhem.

The bear sounds were coming from every direction now. The first pickup truck tore out of the camp. A group of bears raced ahead of it, heading straight for one of Kirby's speakers. Spencer knew that Ro Ro, Raymond, Marguerite, Zoe, and John Shirley were each stationed at a speaker, and Kate and Kenny were together at the last one. As soon as the free bears in the woods heard the army coming, they'd take off running as fast as they could away from camp. Pam's army would follow the scent, racing farther and farther away.

Three more pickup trucks accelerated out of view, heading in three separate directions. Bears from Pam's army ran out ahead of each one.

"It's working!" Spencer whispered as the rest of the pickup trucks and bears took off, baited by the fake bear cries. Now Pam's army was splintered, broken up into six groups and being led away from the camp by the free bears. Kirby started to lower the volume on all six of her speakers, making the recorded bears sound as though they were moving farther away, too.

"Let's go," B.D. said as soon as the trucks and bears were all out of sight and Pam had disappeared back into his trailer.

"Darwin, you're going to stay here, with Kirby," Dora said gently to the cub, who was leaning up against her. "You'll be able to see us from here, all right?"

"Okay," Darwin said after a second. He wobbled across a few branches to settle himself beside Kirby and fixed his wide little eyes on Dora the second he was seated, as though reminding her not to leave his sight.

"Here, Spencer," Dora said once they'd climbed down, lowering her head for Spencer to take her BEAR-COM.

"See you in there." Spencer removed the translating device and quickly tucked it into his mission pack. Dora grunted something to B.D., then padded toward the camp. It would be her job to distract the only person left standing between them and Bearhaven's captive bears: Pam.

Spencer, B.D., and Aldo took off into the woods. They had to be ready at Pam's trailer when Dora arrived. Spencer could feel the adrenaline start to pump into his veins as they crept closer and closer to Pam's mobile lair. B.D. split off to take up his post on one side of the trailer, while Aldo and Spencer crept up to the other side, stationing themselves just below the window to Pam's bedroom.

Thump! Spencer jumped. It sounded like something

soft had hit the trailer. *Dora must be headbutting the door,* he thought. Aldo's ears twitched toward the window above them, as though he was listening to something inside.

Creak! Spencer listened as the door to the trailer opened, but just a crack, he guessed, from the sound. Dora huffed. Then—*bang!*—the door was thrown wide.

"Dora!" Pam exclaimed. "You escaped!"

Aldo immediately crouched down. Spencer climbed onto the bear's back and grabbed hold of the window.

"A little higher," he whispered, and felt Aldo rise up a few inches. Spencer wobbled but held tight to the window. He slipped the screen out of place and then climbed inside, tumbling awkwardly onto the bed.

"I knew you wouldn't let them take you from me, Dora," Pam cooed happily outside, and Spencer relaxed. Pam hadn't heard his fall from the window. He scrambled off the bed and silent-walked through the room and down the short hallway. When he reached the kitchen, he dropped to his knees and crawled into the trailer's main room. Through the trailer's open door, Spencer could see Pam petting Dora affectionately, his back to Spencer.

"I knew you'd be back. Nobody treats you as well as I do, Dora," Pam murmured. "Nobody else knows how valuable you are."

Spencer cringed at Pam's words, then forced himself to ignore Pam altogether. Spencer had to stay focused on searching the room for the master remote Dora had told him would be here somewhere. It could override whatever Margo was directing the bears to do. If Spencer could just get his hands on it now, he'd be able to stop the microchipped bears from attacking, leaving Pam's army useless.

Spencer looked across the room to Evarita. Her hands were wrapped around the bars of her cell as her eyes flicked back and forth between the trailer's open doorway and Spencer, crouched on the ground just a few feet behind.

"Where's the remote?" Spencer mouthed to her, motioning with his hands at the same time. Evarita shook her head, staring at him. She didn't know what he was trying to say. Spencer would have to find it himself. He scanned the long black desk, but part of it was blocked from his view by Pam's throne. He'd have to get closer, but getting closer meant crossing the open room . . .

Spencer glanced out the door. Pam was still absorbed in Dora's homecoming. If Spencer was going to get closer, he had to go now. He crawled forward slowly, afraid to make even the tiniest sound. He could feel Evarita's eyes bearing down on him from inside her cell. When he reached the desk, he poked his head up over its edge. He spotted a notebook, with a gold pen resting on top of it, but no remote.

Where is it?! It has to be here! Spencer crawled into the dark under the desk. He had to think. What about the set of drawers to his right?

Slowly, Spencer reached an arm out from under the desk and rolled the top drawer open. Luckily, it didn't make a sound, but from under the desk, Spencer couldn't see inside the drawer. He tried to crawl closer, but his mission pack got hooked on the armrest of Pam's throne. *Come on!* Spencer tried to pull his mission pack free so that he could look inside the drawer, but when he tugged, the throne started to tip backward.

Spencer heard Evarita stifle a gasp as he lunged out from under the desk, trying to stop Pam's throne from falling.

But he was too late.

30

CRASH!

The sound of Pam's heavy throne hitting the floor echoed through the trailer. For a second, everything seemed to move in slow motion. Spencer stood frozen in place, every muscle in his body tense as he watched Pam whirl around.

Pam let out an earsplitting shriek of anger just as something on the armrest of the overturned throne caught Spencer's eye. It was the remote. Four bear claw prongs held it in place on the side of the armrest.

"You again!" Pam howled furiously. He rushed into the trailer with Dora close behind him, his clawed hands reaching for Spencer.

"No," Spencer whispered, his eyes returning to the remote. If he could get it now, he still might have some chance—Spencer dove for the remote at the same moment that Pam grabbed for him.

"No you don't!" Pam screamed.

"Ahh!" Spencer's hand brushed the remote, but his arm was yanked away. Pam's nails dug into Spencer's flesh through his T-shirt. "Let go of me!" Spencer yelled. To his surprise, Pam did let go but not without giving Spencer a hard shove. Spencer stumbled backward, then felt hands break his fall.

"Leave him alone!" Evarita yelled from behind Spencer as she pulled him to his feet, her hands reaching through the bars of her cell.

"Quiet! You can't do him any good from in there," Pam spat at Evarita, then turned his glare on Spencer. Spencer gulped. His back was pressed against Evarita's cell, and Pam was between him and the trailer's open door. Spencer had nowhere to run. Dora stepped up to Pam's side and Spencer could feel her eyes on him, but he was afraid to look away from Pam. There was no telling what Pam planned to do next.

"I'm getting really sick of you, Spencer Plain," Pam said, his eyes narrowed.

"Then I'll just get out of your way," Spencer answered, but he could hear his voice shaking. He took a step toward Pam, trying to get to the door.

"Oh, no you don't!" Pam shrilled. "You're not going anywhere except right into that cell," Pam practically snarled. Out of the corner of his eye, Spencer saw Dora bristle at the threatening tone of Pam's voice. Pam snatched something out of his open desk drawer and took a hasty step toward Spencer, reaching out to grab him.

Pop! Pop! Dora stepped in between Pam and Spencer. She turned on Pam, forcing him to take a step back.

"Dora! Stay away from him! What are you . . ." Pam started, then realized what was going on. "You're *protecting* this pest?!" he cried, the fury rising in his voice. "You turned my own bear on me?!" Pam screamed, turning to Spencer. "HOW DARE YOU?!" Dora rose up onto her hind legs, shielding Spencer even more. "You might as well have *killed her.*" Pam's voice dropped dangerously low. Goose bumps rose on Spencer's arms.

Spencer sidestepped Dora. "I didn't turn her on you," he shouted. "You did that all by yourself when you took her cub away!"

"She's worthless to me now," Pam spat, ignoring Spencer's accusation. "You hear me?" he shouted at Dora. Pam grabbed something else from the open desk drawer.

"No!" Spencer shouted when he saw it. It was a handheld tranquilizer gun, with a single dart poised in it. Pam had one shot, and he was aiming it straight at Dora's chest. Dora dropped to all fours and shuffled backward, but after just a few paces, she hit Evarita's cell.

"You did this, Plain," Pam said. "By turning her on me, you did this. Remember that."

"No!" Spencer lunged forward. He grabbed the notebook from the desk, sending the gold pen flying. Then, just as Pam pulled the trigger, Spencer hurled the notebook in front of Dora. The tranquilizer dart glanced off the notebook and ricocheted to the floor.

"Ugh!" Pam scrambled to retrieve the dart, and Spencer saw his opportunity. He ran forward and crashed into Pam just as Pam's hand closed around the dart, knocking him to the floor.

"*Grauk!* Dora!" Spencer shouted the bears' word for "go." He lunged over to Pam's throne and grabbed the remote, then took a flying leap and jumped over Pam, making for the door. When Spencer's feet hit the floor, he felt something wrap around his ankle. "Ahhh!" he cried, feeling Pam's nails pierce his skin. Spencer fell to the ground. He tried to scramble away, but Pam wouldn't let go.

"Let him go!" Evarita cried.

Dora huffed and stepped forward until she was standing over Pam, huffing and snapping.

"Let go!" Spencer yelled. He tried to kick Pam with his other foot, but Pam reached out to grab that leg, too. "Ahhh!" Spencer felt something break the skin on his second ankle. He thought it was Pam's sharpened fingernails, but then everything went dark.

31

Spencer woke up in the TUBE's medical car with Darwin snuffling at his ear and Kate peering at him from only a few feet away.

"He's awake!" Kate cheered. A second later, Spencer was surrounded. The free bears crowded around Spencer's bear-sized hospital bed.

"Oh, thank goodness," Ro Ro murmured, looking Spencer over.

"How are you feeling, little man?" Aldo asked. Spencer started to sit up. *What happened?* It was obvious that all the free bears had been waiting in the medical car for him to wake up . . . but how had he gotten here? The last thing he remembered he was in Pam's trailer, trying to escape the horrible man's grasp around his ankle.

"Not yet, Spencer," Marguerite said, reaching out a paw to gently stop him from sitting up. "Stay where you are for a few more minutes. I just gave you a shot to reverse the—"

Marguerite stopped at the sound of someone rushing into the medical car.

Reverse what?! Spencer wondered, his mind racing.

"What's going on?" Evarita called over the crowd.

"Evarita?" Spencer watched B.D. and John Shirley step aside to allow Evarita to reach the hospital bed.

"You're awake!" Evarita exclaimed as soon as she saw him. She stretched across Kate to give Spencer a big hug.

"You're here!" Spencer answered. "What happened?" he finally managed to ask.

"You were tranquilized!" Kenny piped up. "Just like me!"

"Pam *tranquilized* me?!" Spencer could hardly believe it.

"Yes, with the loose tranquilizer dart," Dora explained.

"How did we get away?" Spencer asked, looking from Dora to Evarita. With Spencer unconscious and Evarita locked up, he couldn't imagine how they'd all escaped Pam's trailer.

"Dora dragged Pam off you," Evarita said. "And I'd gotten the lock-picking kit out of your mission pack while you were pressed up against my cell."

"And I called B.D. and Aldo in," Dora said. "Between the four of us, we managed to lock Pam in the cell."

"Then we stole the Hummer and got out of there," Evarita finished.

"Wow," Spencer said, impressed. "I'm sorry I missed it." He would have loved to see Pam locked up and Evarita hot-wiring a Hummer. "What about—" Spencer started, unsure of the mission's outcome. Had the free bears managed to finish it without him? But Aldo cut him off.

"We're just glad you're all right," Aldo said. The rest of the free bears nodded their agreement, but Spencer could tell by their faces that the mission had been a failure.

"We outran the bear army, Spencer," Kate reported proudly. "The plan was working—"

"Until the end," Zoe cut in.

"We're still the only free bears," Raymond said simply.

"I'm sorry." Spencer looked down at his bandaged ankles. He'd failed. He'd let the free bears down. If he'd just found the remote faster . . .

"Don't worry," Darwin said, leaning against Spencer. "We'll go home to Bearhaven now. My family will come there."

Spencer looked down at the little cub. The tips of the white crown emblazoned on his chest were just visible. "But your family is here, Darwin," he said, trying to make sense of what the cub meant.

Darwin looked around the circle of faces surrounding him and Spencer. "No, only Mom, Uncle B.D., Uncle John Shirley, and Zoe are here," the cub said.

Zoe? Spencer thought. Zoe was related to Pinky, they all knew that. But was she somehow a Benally, too? It didn't seem likely.

Dora, B.D., and John Shirley all looked at Zoe, as though hoping she could explain, but Zoe looked bewildered and shook her head back at them.

"Marguerite," Evarita said quietly. "Where's Spencer's mission pack?"

Marguerite left the circle for a moment, then returned with the pack in her mouth. She rested it on the hospital bed by Spencer's legs. Evarita reached over and unzipped the top, then dug around until she pulled out a white Post-it note.

"What's that?" Spencer asked. He was sure he hadn't packed the small piece of paper for the mission to Pam's camp. Evarita started to unfold the paper, revealing it wasn't a Post-it note at all, but a packet of full-sized pages.

"It's about Darwin," Evarita said. "I got lucky and was able to slip it off Pam's desk yesterday when his back was turned. Then, when Spencer was up against my cell, I put it in his mission pack."

"What does it say?" Dora asked hastily. "What about Darwin?"

"I haven't had time to read it yet," Evarita said. She laid the pages flat on Spencer's bed and smoothed them out. This time, when Spencer moved to sit up Marguerite didn't try to stop him. Spencer leaned over the papers, studying them with Evarita. "It says 'Darwin's Gene Selections' at the top and seems to be a list of all the bears in the bear army," Evarita went on. "There are eighty-eight animals listed here, by ID numbers."

Spencer scanned the list that stretched for several pages.

4201: eye color

4202: snout structure

4203: fur texture

"What's a gene?" Kate asked.

"Genes are little pieces of information that are passed down from a parent to a child, or a cub," Evarita explained as she pored over the stolen papers. "Your genes decide what your characteristics will be like, like what color hair—I mean, fur—you'll have."

"If they come from your parents, why would Darwin's be selected?" Spencer asked, looking again at the title on the paper, *Darwin's Gene Selections*. "And what does that have to do with the rest of the bear army?"

"My family," Darwin said. Evarita looked up at him.

"Darwin, is the bear army your family?" she asked.

"Yes, my big family," the cub answered, then buried his face in Spencer's side, as though trying to hide from the attention.

"Evarita, what does all of this mean?" B.D. spoke up.

Evarita took a deep breath. "I think it means that Pam used the bears in the bear army to handpick Darwin's genes. Pam must have found scientists to help him create what he thought was the perfect bear cub, using the qualities the bears in the bear army already had, and combining the ones he determined to be the best from each."

"That would explain why Darwin's so valuable to Pam," Spencer said.

"And why Darwin feels like the bear army is his family, too," Dora answered.

"Right. Darwin technically has a little bit of all of them in him." Evarita folded the papers back up. Everyone looked at Darwin.

"We'll go home to Bearhaven now?" the cub asked.

The room fell silent.

"You know, he might be on to something," John Shirley said, speaking up for the first time.

"You think we should go back to Bearhaven?" Spencer asked. He felt like his head was spinning with the new information about Darwin. For the first time in days, thinking about what they should do next had been the furthest thing from his mind.

John Shirley nodded. "And let them come to us."

"Fight Pam on familiar territory," B.D. said thoughtfully. "It's not a bad idea."

"So we're going to try again?" Zoe asked tentatively.

Dora looked at her. "If the bear army is Darwin's family, they're our family, too," she said. "This isn't just about Bearhaven's bears anymore. Pam has done far too much damage to bears that all of us care about, and bears we don't even know yet. It's time he was stopped, and all our bears went free. Once and for all."

Spencer jumped at the sound of the medical car door opening.

"You guys, this train is so cool. I can't believe all the high-tech equipment you bears have. Where do you get all this stuff anyway?" It was Kirby. Everyone turned to look at her, clearing a space for Spencer to see his friend. "Is Spencer awake?"

"Hey, Kirby," Spencer called.

"What did I miss?" Kirby asked, seeming to notice for the first time that the mood in the medical car was serious.

"We're going to try again," Spencer said. "We're going to stop Pam. Once and for all."

32

"It could be worse," Raymond said, breaking the silence in a heavy voice.

"Could it?" Marguerite asked. Spencer wasn't sure. Even he had been shocked to see Bearhaven when they'd all reached the hilltop overlooking the valley.

The abandoned valley was blackened, a ghost of the Bearhaven they'd evacuated only a week ago. The buildings were decimated, but they weren't gone completely, maybe because of the rain on the night of the fire. Instead, they were now half-crumbled walls surrounding piles of rubble.

The rings of houses that Spencer was so used to seeing glow like an inviting honeycomb now looked like a maze of soot-covered ruins. The center of Bearhaven was nothing more than a menacing looking pen, enclosed on three sides by fire-eaten structures. Only the Lab was fully intact.

"It must've been cool," Kirby whispered to Spencer.

"It was the coolest," he whispered back.

"All right, we have work to do," B.D. said. The bear's tone was gruff, but Spencer guessed it was because B.D. couldn't stand to linger over the damage Pam had done any longer. And they *did* have work to do. A lot of work.

Before leaving the TUBE, Spencer, B.D., Evarita, Kirby, and the rest of the free bears had come up with a plan. Spencer was sure this one would work, but they had to act fast. Margo, Ivan, and Pam's guards would have returned to camp by now and released Pam from his cell. Spencer guessed Pam wouldn't wait long before setting out to get his revenge and capture every single bear he could. They had to be ready when he got here.

B.D. stepped out in front of everyone and turned to face them, his back to Bearhaven. "You all know where you're supposed to go first?" he asked, looking around.

"I'm off to see what I can find at the café," Raymond said. "I'll prepare something nice and *ripe* for perfume." Spencer smiled. He couldn't wait to smell what Raymond made for the bears to wear to mask their scents and hopefully throw off the bear army.

"Aldo, Ro Ro, Kenny, Zoe, Dora, and John Shirley," B.D. said, looking down the line. "You're all with me. We have to turn that destruction"—B.D. nodded in the direction of the bears' burnt homes and the scorched pathways that wound between them—"into a trap as quickly as possible."

"I'm going to help you all move some boulders with the Hummer," Evarita said. "Then go to the Lab to see if I can get a call out to Jane, Shane, and Mark."

"And Kate, Kirby, and Darwin will go to the Lab with me," Spencer spoke up. "Kirby will try to repair the surveillance system, and Darwin and I will get Kate ready." Out of the corner of his eye, Spencer saw Kate shift uneasily beside him. She'd agreed to play an important and dangerous part in the plan, but she looked as if she was still nervous about what she would have to do.

"We'll all meet in the center of Bearhaven as soon as we can." With that, the Head of the Guard turned and charged down the hill, heading for the Bear Guard training field. The group of bears assigned to trap duty ran to catch up.

"Want a ride to the Lab?" Evarita asked. "I can speed you four over there, then meet everyone else at the training field."

Spencer eyed the stolen black Hummer parked just behind them.

"We sure do!" Kate answered before anyone else could. "But don't forget, we need to make one quick stop on the way so I can get ready!"

Spencer, Kate, and Darwin stood in the Bear Guard supply closet. Spencer was still having trouble looking at Kate without cracking up. In order to play her part in the plan, the one quick stop she'd needed to make on the way to the Lab was at the schoolhouse, where she'd leaped from the Hummer and dove into the pile of ash and soot that had once been her classroom. Now she was covered head to toe in the black stuff, her fur stained and coated so that she matched Darwin.

"You look like me!" Darwin said again, doing a lap around Kate as Spencer searched the shelves for medical supplies.

"I know!" Kate exclaimed. "That's the whole point. I'm supposed to look like you!"

Spencer grabbed a stack of first aid kits and dropped

them on the floor in front of Kate. He sat down and started to pull out all the white medical tape he could find.

"All right." Spencer looked back and forth between Darwin and Kate, who were both sitting back on their haunches, waiting for him. "This might pull at your fur a little," he said to Kate, then cut a strip of white medical tape off the roll. He pressed the tape against Kate's chest, so that it looked like she had a pure white blaze mark. He cut another strip and placed it directly beside the first.

"How does it look?" Kate asked after a few more strips of tape had been added to her fake blaze mark. Spencer leaned back and looked at the real crown-shaped blaze mark on Darwin.

"We're getting close," he said, then added points to Kate's fake crown, until a few minutes later he decided his work was done. Two black cubs looked back at him, each with a white crown on their chest. Kate's wasn't perfect, but Kate was also twice Darwin's size. Even so, from a distance, Spencer was sure she'd be mistaken for Darwin, especially if Dora was by her side, and that would be enough, he hoped, to convince Pam and bait him down into the valley.

"Two Darwins!" Darwin said, examining Kate as Spencer slipped an extra roll of medical tape into his mission pack for later, in case Kate's crown came loose.

"One Darwin," Spencer answered. "And one Kate in disguise."

Spencer was about to lead the way out of the supply closet when the trunk on the back wall caught his eye. He strode over to it.

If we're going to defeat Pam on our turf, he thought,

we should mark it as our turf. He flipped open the lid of the trunk. Bearhaven's two flags were still folded neatly inside.

"Kate," he said, pulling out the first flag.

"Yeah?"

"What does the picture on the Bearhaven flag mean?" he asked, holding it up. It was all black except for the silver image of a crown resting on an upraised bear claw.

"It means freedom," Kate answered. "As bears, we are meant to be our own masters and rule over our own lives," she went on, as though reciting lines she'd learned in school.

Spencer looked back and forth between Darwin and Kate. He couldn't help but think it wasn't just a coincidence that Pam's prized cub was marked with the crown, Bearhaven's symbol of freedom. Darwin, just like all the other bears in Pam's captivity, was meant to be free. He had the symbol on his chest to prove it.

Spencer tucked the Bearhaven flag under his arm, even more determined now to have it flying over the valley when he and the free bears defeated Pam.

Spencer let the lid of the trunk fall shut with a quiet thud, hiding Dora's flag, the second flag in the trunk, from view. There would be time later for B.D. to explain to his sister how Bearhaven had honored her with that second flag since the beginning.

"We'd better get going," Spencer said.

33

"Kirby, can you hear me?" Spencer asked, a hand on the Ear-COM in his ear. He and Kate were on their way to the center of Bearhaven. They'd left Kirby hard at work in the Lab's surveillance room trying to repair the equipment Zoc had broken on her rampage. Darwin would stay with Kirby. The last Spencer had seen the cub, he was curled up on a wool blanket beside Kirby, gnawing on Raymond's fuel bars.

"I can hear you!" Kirby's voice shouted into Spencer's ear. Spencer flinched. When he had fitted Kirby with an Ear-COM, another one of Bearhaven's cool pieces of technology, he'd forgotten to mention that she wouldn't have to yell. The Ear-COM would pick up her regular voice, allowing them to communicate throughout the mission.

"Okay," he said, hoping he hadn't forgotten to tell her anything else about how to use the special operative gear. "But you can just talk in your normal voice."

"Right. Got it. No problem," Kirby answered, then fell silent. Spencer guessed she was poring over wires and tools now, racing to get the camera at Bearhaven's entrance up and running.

"We'll reconnect when the team is ready," Spencer said, before cutting off his communication with Kirby. "Disconnect."

"Do I still look like Darwin?" Kate asked in an anxious whisper as they passed the meetinghouse and turned into the center of Bearhaven.

"Just like him," Spencer reassured the cub.

"Kate! Spencer!" Aldo called from the group waiting by the flagpoles. "Kate, you look great," Aldo said once Spencer and Kate had reached everyone. They were the last to arrive.

"What's that *smell*?" Kate asked. Spencer looked around the group of bears. There did seem to be an unusual smell coming from them, now that he thought of it.

"I call it eau de cabbage," Raymond said with an unexpectedly cheerful flourish, stepping forward for Spencer and Kate to get a good whiff of him. He smelled a little bit like stinky feet, and not at all like a bear. *Right*, Spencer thought, *the protective perfume.*

"Boiled cabbage water," Ro Ro explained. Kenny shot her a sour look.

"How come the other bears don't have to wear it?" he asked crankily, obviously not a fan of his new odor.

B.D. stepped out of the group of bears, breaking off his conversation with Dora and Evarita. "Only the bears who will be in the trap need to be able to throw Pam's bears off with the cabbage smell, Kenny. It's to protect you." The cub pawed at the ground but didn't dare talk back to the

Head of the Guard. "Spencer, did you bring Ear-COMs for Evarita and me?" he asked.

"Yes," Spencer answered, digging the devices out of the front pocket of his mission pack.

"Good," B.D. answered, bowing his great furry head down in front of Spencer. "Everyone else will have their BEAR-COMs, and this way, we'll have someone stationed at each place to communicate." Spencer fit the larger of the two Ear-COMs into B.D.'s ear, then passed the second one to Evarita. "The trap is ready," B.D. updated Spencer and Kate. "It's a maze in there, thanks to the fire, and we've blocked every entrance but one. Once the guards drive in, Aldo and Spencer will be right behind them and will block the last entrance so the trucks will be trapped. Then our five bears inside will stall them, leading them through the maze in all different directions. Hopefully, we'll be able to get Pam down into the valley using Kate posing as Darwin as bait, and ambush him before things get too intense in the trap."

"Then I'll neutralize the bear army? With the remote?" Spencer said.

"Yes, as soon as you get the remote," B.D. said, sitting back on his haunches. "And let's remember, all of us"— B.D. scanned the group—"today, we're fighting to save our families and our friends. Both those we've known as members of the Bearhaven community, and those we don't know yet—the members of Pam's bear army." All the bears nodded and murmured their agreement. Spencer watched B.D. carefully. He'd never seen the Head of the Guard speak this way, but he knew this mission—this *battle*—wasn't like anything B.D. had ever led before. "It could just as easily have been any of us microchipped and under Pam's control. These aren't our enemies we're fighting against—they're our brothers and sisters." B.D. fell silent as the free bears murmured their agreement.

"B.D.?" Spencer pulled the Bearhaven flag out from under one arm. "I brought this."

"Bearhaven's flag?" Marguerite asked, eyeing the folds of black fabric curiously.

"To mark our territory," John Shirley said with a smile.

"To show them what we stand for," Aldo corrected.

"Freedom for all bears." Spencer unfurled the flag, revealing the image of the crown on the upraised bear claw. B.D. nodded his approval, and Spencer walked over to the flagpole and raised Bearhaven's flag. When it had reached the top of the flagpole, Spencer stepped back and watched the flag drift in the breeze, dark against the bright blue afternoon sky.

"Abragan," B.D. said. Spencer turned back to the Head of the Guard to find that B.D. had switched off his BEAR-COM.

"For the bears," everyone answered, repeating Bearhaven's official mission send-off.

B.D. lifted a claw back to his BEAR-COM and turned it on again. "Team," he said, connecting his Ear-COM to Evarita's, Spencer's, and Kirby's.

"Hello?" Kirby's voice immediately rang loudly into Spencer's ear. "I was just about to call you! They're coming!"

34

Spencer and Aldo hid behind a boulder at the entrance to the trap.

"There they are," Aldo panted, still trying to catch his breath after Kirby's alert made them sprint to get into position. His eyes were glued to the army of microchipped bears on the hilltop overlooking Bearhaven.

"They look even scarier than last time," Spencer whispered. He had a pair of binoculars pressed against his eyes as he peered out from under the curve of the boulder.

After Kirby had announced that Pam and his army were at the outskirts of Bearhaven, the free bears had sprung into action. Now Kenny, Ro Ro, Raymond, Marguerite, and Zoe were at their places inside the trap. Evarita was at a hideout overlooking the bears' now-burned homes. It was her job to keep everyone updated on the situation inside the trap—the movements of the bear army and of the free bears—paying special attention to Margo and Ivan.

B.D. and John Shirley were taking cover behind two of the remaining boulders in the Bear Guard training field. And Dora and Kate were hidden behind the rubble of Raymond's Café, where Aldo and Spencer would meet them once they closed the entrance to the trap.

"Do you see Pam?" Aldo asked.

"Not yet." Spencer scanned the hilltop. The bears had fanned out, and were staring down into the valley. Through the binoculars, they seemed ferocious, and impatient. They weren't the stiff, robotic army he was used to. Spencer looked away. He didn't know what the change in the behavior of the microchipped bears could mean, but he didn't want to bother Aldo with it, in case he was wrong.

The pickup trucks had pulled to either side of the bear army. Spencer could just see the groups of glaring, tranquilizer-toting guards that were piled into each one. He spotted Margo and Ivan in their own truck, then one last pickup truck sped onto the hill. It veered in front of the rows of bears and trucks, then slammed to a stop on the very top of the ridge, in front of the army. A black crown had been spray-painted onto the hood of the silver truck. It glistened in the sun, like it might still be wet.

"That's him," he said, his mouth suddenly dry. Pam was behind the wheel of the final pickup truck, and he looked furious—the usual satisfied smirk was gone.

"Is anyone in the truck with him?" Aldo asked.

"No," Spencer answered.

"Good," Aldo said. "He'll probably command things from up there as we thought he would."

"Yeah," Spencer answered. "I bet he doesn't want to come close enough to get into any trouble himself, after what happened in the trailer."

"Doesn't want to end up in a cage again," Aldo muttered.

"Team," Evarita said, her voice in Spencer's ear. "The bears in the trap are starting to move."

Spencer ducked back behind the boulder and tucked his binoculars into his mission pack.

"The bears inside are moving," he said to Aldo. From the hilltop where Pam was, it would look like the bears inside Bearhaven were caught by surprise and running for their lives, trying to take cover in what was left of their homes.

Vroom!

Vroom!

Vroom!

The sounds of trucks accelerating filled the valley, heading straight for where he and Aldo were hiding. The ground under Spencer started to shake with the heavy footsteps of eighty-seven running bears.

"They're getting closer," he whispered.

"We can't get in this way!" a guard shouted. "Go around the side!"

Spencer and Aldo pressed themselves against the boulder. The one open entrance to the trap didn't face the hill. Instead, it was around the side of the arching outer border of the bears' homes so that Pam wouldn't be able to see any movement when Aldo and Spencer sealed it shut. The bears and guards would find it any second now.

"Follow the bears! They'll find the way in!" shouted a guard.

The sounds of army bears running, jaw popping, and huffing was suddenly only inches away. They thundered past, just on the other side of Spencer and Aldo's boulder.

"They found an opening!" another guard called. "Over here!"

Spencer listened as the first truck sped past. The plan was working! Aside from the entrance Spencer and Aldo hid beside now, every other pathway into the network of bears' homes had been barricaded with layers of burned debris and boulders. B.D. and his team had created a barricaded circle.

"They're all in." Evarita's voice interrupted Spencer's thoughts. "All but one truck that stayed behind. I think it's Pam."

"Perfect," Spencer whispered.

"Spencer," B.D.'s voice chimed in. "Tell Aldo to seal the entrance."

"Aldo," Spencer said, knowing his words would carry through his Ear-COM to B.D., too. "We can close it up."

Aldo rose onto his hind legs, placing his front two paws onto the boulder, and started to push. The boulder was twice the bear's size, and it looked like every muscle in the bear's body was straining. Spencer leaped to his feet. He joined Aldo in pushing, and the boulder started to roll. It moved slowly, but it didn't need to go far. After Spencer and Aldo had rolled the boulder one full rotation, they hurried around to the other side of the entrance, where another boulder waited. Again, Aldo braced his front paws on the enormous rock and started to muscle it forward. Spencer took his place beside the bear, doing what he could to help.

Crunch! The second boulder hit the first.

"The trap's closed!" Spencer exclaimed. Aldo crouched down beside him, already ready to move on to the next stage in the plan, and Spencer climbed onto the bear's back. "We're heading for Kate and Dora now!"

Aldo took off running. They'd have to go the long way to Raymond's Café to avoid being seen by Pam, but at the pace Aldo was running, it wouldn't take long.

"How are things in the trap, Evarita?" Spencer asked as they ran, wishing he could get a view inside to see the game of cat and mouse the free bears were playing with Pam's army.

"All good here!" Evarita answered. "Our bears have spread out, and they're staying ahead of the army."

"Great!" Spencer called back.

"What did she say?" Aldo asked when they reached Raymond's. He padded over to where Kate and Dora were waiting behind the only wall of the café that was still standing.

"Everything's going according to plan so far," Spencer answered once Kate and Dora were within earshot.

"Ready to be the star of the show, Kate?" Aldo asked his little sister.

"I'm ready," Kate said, puffing up her chest to show off the temporary blaze mark on her soot-stained fur.

Dora padded over to the far edge of the wall and looked out, as though judging the distance from where they all stood now, to the Bear Guard training field. "We go first," she said, reviewing the plan. "Then you two follow once Pam's in the valley, trying to get me and Kate?" She looked back and forth between Spencer and Aldo.

"Yes," Aldo confirmed. "And B.D. and John Shirley are

already in the training field, ready to ambush Pam as soon as you lead him there."

"All right." Dora nodded solemnly. "Kate?"

Kate stepped in beside Dora. "For the bears?" she said nervously, turning back to Spencer and Aldo.

"For the bears," they both replied.

"Well then, let's go!" Kate exclaimed, and took off running. Dora lunged forward, falling into line with Kate as they started the long sprint to the Bear Guard training field.

35

"Margo! Guards!" Pam continued to holler out over Bearhaven through his golden megaphone.

"They can't get out!" Evarita reported through the Ear-COMs. "The guards and Margo and Ivan can't even find the entrance they came through. It's working!"

Yes! Spencer imagined the pickup trucks tearing around the pathways, lost in the maze of the bears' burned homes.

"Has he moved?" B.D. asked.

"Not yet," Spencer answered. He was crouched down, peeking through the one singed window in Raymond's last remaining wall, his eyes glued to Pam on the hilltop. "He's jumping around outside his truck." *Come on,* Spencer thought. *Go after them!*

"We're going to lose them!" Pam howled at the top of his lungs.

"He's getting back in the truck!" Spencer exclaimed as he watched Pam hurry around the side of his truck, tear open the door, toss the megaphone inside, and scramble into the driver's seat.

Vroom!

"And he's taking the bait!" Spencer cheered. Pam's truck

accelerated down the hill heading for Dora and Kate, who were now halfway to the Bear Guard training field.

"Let's get ready, then," Aldo said, crouching down. Spencer could feel his heart starting to race as he climbed back onto the bear's back.

"Something's wrong!" Evarita's voice suddenly chimed in.

"What?" Spencer asked.

"What is it?" B.D. said at the same time.

Spencer leaned over so that he could get a view through the window again. Pam was still speeding toward Dora and Kate.

"The bear army is attacking!" Evarita shouted. "They've trapped Kenny and Ro Ro!"

"What do you mean, they're attacking?!" Spencer cried. "They're not supposed to injure our bears!"

"They're attacking!" Evarita repeated. "Raymond's hurt!"

"Spencer," B.D. barked. "Where's Pam now?"

Spencer looked back through the window, but the pickup truck was gone. "Where's Pam?" he whispered.

"He's gaining on them," Aldo answered, trotting to the very edge of the wall. "We should go." Pam had already crossed the center of the valley and had fallen in behind Dora and Kate, blocking Spencer's and Aldo's view of the two bears.

"B.D., he's coming toward you now!" Spencer updated the Head of the Guard. "And so are we!" Aldo took that as the cue to go and launched forward, breaking into a sprint.

"Hurry," Evarita urged them through the Ear-COM. "It's bad in here."

"Hurry, Aldo!" Spencer repeated the message. "The

bears in the trap are in trouble." Spencer felt Aldo strain to go faster. They were already gaining on Pam's truck. Aldo veered off to the side so that he and Spencer could get a view of the Bear Guard training field up ahead. Four boulders were arranged in an arch. Spencer knew B.D. and John Shirley were behind two of them, and Kate and Dora would lead Pam straight into that semicircle of rocks. Aldo and Spencer would follow them in.

Spencer put his head down, pressing his face into the black-and-brown fur at the back of Aldo's head. *We can do this,* he thought. *We ambush him. I grab the remote. We ambush him. I grab the remote,* Spencer told himself, over and over again. The last thing he wanted to do was mess up his part in taking Pam down. Spencer wished he could reach for his jade bear now. He was going to need all the bravery he could get.

"Almost there," Aldo said, and Spencer looked up. Kate and Dora were entering the ring of boulders, with Pam just behind them, and Spencer and Aldo a few yards behind Pam. "You ready, little man?" Aldo asked.

Spencer gulped. "Ready," he said.

Kate and Dora slowed down inside the ring of boulders and spun around to face Pam, as though trapped. Pam slammed on his brakes and skidded to a halt.

"What is this?!" Pam shouted just as Aldo slowed his pace to a silent trot and snuck up to the side of the pickup truck. He stopped alongside it, and Spencer carefully stood on the bear's back, then stepped into the bed of the truck. "That's not my cub!" Pam shrieked, his eyes on Kate. "WHERE IS MY CUB?!"

Spencer crouched down and crawled to the truck's back window. He couldn't let Pam see him until Aldo, B.D., and John Shirley had attacked, or else Pam would know they were after the remote and speed away. Spencer peeked through the window. Dora and Kate were both staring wide-eyed at Pam, as though frozen in place by fear. By now, Aldo would be poised by the passenger-side door, ready to attack as soon as he saw B.D. Everyone was in position.

"Ughhh!" Pam let out another howl of frustration.

"Now, B.D.!" Spencer whispered.

B.D. and John Shirley came tearing out from behind two boulders, heading straight for Pam, just as Pam gunned his engine.

What's he doing?! Spencer started to panic.

"You betrayed me one too many times, Dora!" Pam shouted, then slammed on the gas. Spencer was thrown backward.

"No!" he shouted, grabbing desperately for the side of the truck. He regained his balance and then his view of Dora and Kate. Pam was heading straight for them. Kate sprinted away, taking cover behind the closest boulder. But Dora didn't move. Her eyes were locked on Pam, and they were filled with terror. She stumbled backward and bumped up against the boulder behind her. Out of the corner of his eye, Spencer saw B.D. change direction. He was heading for his sister now, but Pam was only seconds from slamming into her.

"Run, Dora!" Spencer screamed. Pam's eyes flicked to his rearview mirror and met Spencer's. The truck didn't slow down.

"I told you, you might as well have killed her!" Pam cried, his eyes still on Spencer.

Bang! The truck slammed into something and crashed to a stop.

"No!" Spencer was thrown backward again. He scrambled to his feet and leaped out of the pickup truck. The first thing he saw was Dora. She was at the front of the truck, but to one side and standing. It wasn't her that the truck had hit. Relief started to flood over Spencer, but then he realized Dora was bending over a huge black mass on the ground in front of the pickup truck's smashed hood. Spencer took a step forward, terrified of what he'd find when he got a better view.

"No," he gasped when finally he could make out the figure on the ground. "B.D.," he whispered. His voice choked as he stumbled closer. B.D. didn't move.

36

"Evarita!" Spencer gasped into his Ear-COM. He was bent over B.D., trying to ignore the mayhem around him. "B.D.'s hurt. He can't walk. Can you bring the Hummer?"

"I'm coming," Evarita answered immediately.

"Spencer, can I help?" Kirby chimed in. Spencer could hardly hear her over the furious banging behind him.

Evarita jumped in to answer. "Just keep us updated on what you see, Kirby," she said.

"B.D.," Aldo whispered, his eyes flicking from the unmoving bear on the ground to the attack Dora and John Shirley were making on the pickup truck behind Spencer. "Wake up, B.D., we need you."

Kate stood beside her brother, a few steps back, as though afraid to look at B.D. She looked at Spencer instead, her eyes wide. "He was just trying to protect Dora."

"I know," Spencer answered, trying to swallow the lump in his throat.

Chug, chug, chug . . . Spencer looked over his shoulder. Pam was frantically trying to get his truck to start, but crashing into B.D. seemed to have damaged more than just the pickup truck's hood, and John Shirley and Dora ramming into the sides of the truck weren't helping, either. Spencer didn't want to know what would happen if they got to Pam, but he couldn't help thinking that whatever it was, Pam deserved it.

In the distance, Spencer saw the Hummer speeding toward them.

"B.D.!" Aldo cried.

Spencer turned back to the bear. His eyes were open. He was blinking slowly and wincing in pain. "Don't worry," Spencer said, leaning down over the bear to be sure he would hear. "Evarita's coming to get you out of here. You're going to be fine."

The bear didn't answer, but he tried to move his head, as though searching for something.

"You saved Dora," Kate said, and B.D. gave a small, pained nod.

Spencer heard an engine roaring closer. He glanced over his shoulder just in time to see Evarita fishtail behind the pickup truck. She hit the brakes when she was just a few feet from Spencer, B.D., Aldo, and Kate. Dora and John Shirley continued to rage against Pam's truck, as though they hadn't even noticed Evarita's arrival.

"What happened?!" Evarita shouted as she jumped out of the Hummer and ran over to Spencer's side.

"He got hit by Pam, trying to get Dora out of the way," Spencer said quickly. "Can you take him to the Lab?"

Evarita turned and opened the back of the Hummer. The seats were already down, Spencer guessed from moving boulders around the valley. There was plenty of room for

B.D. inside. "We're going to need help lifting him," Evarita said.

Aldo got to all fours. "Dora! John Shirley!" he yelled over the sounds of their bodies beating against Pam's truck. "We need to move B.D.!"

John Shirley immediately ran over, but Dora continued to throw herself at the side of Pam's truck. An enormous dent had formed in the passenger-side door.

"Dora, now!" Aldo ordered. Dora rushed to B.D.'s side.

"On the count of—" Spencer started as they circled B.D., getting ready to lift him into the Hummer. The sound of the pickup truck's engine coming to life distracted him.

Vroom! Pam had gotten his truck to start at last. He accelerated backward.

"We can't let him get away!" Spencer cried. If Pam got away with the remote now, Spencer and the free bears could lose their chance to stop him.

"Dora, John Shirley, Evarita," Aldo said, taking charge. "Get B.D. to the Lab. Spencer and Kate, let's go." Spencer hopped onto the bear's back, casting one last look at B.D., who was already being lifted into the Hummer. As soon as Spencer had two handfuls of Aldo's fur, Aldo broke into a sprint, taking off after Pam. Kate stayed close behind.

The pickup truck was sputtering, its speed a fraction of what it had been when Pam pursued Dora and Kate to the Bear Guard training field.

"He's not going to make it out of the valley!" Spencer shouted. He was certain the pickup truck was only moments from giving out completely. "Can we get him to drive toward the center of Bearhaven?! Toward the flagpole? We can corner him there!"

"We can try," Aldo called back, then immediately picked up speed. He raced to the dented driver's side door of the truck. Spencer reached out a hand and banged on the window of the moving vehicle. Pam screamed, startled, and veered away from Aldo, Spencer, and Kate. Aldo let him get a few yards ahead, then sped up again. This time, he headed for the passenger-side door. Once he reached it, he let out a ferocious grunt and rammed his shoulder into the pickup truck. Again Pam veered away, changing directions to head straight toward Raymond's Café.

"Team! Everybody! You guys!" Kirby's voice suddenly rang into Spencer's ear. "The bears are climbing out of the trap! They're going over the walls!"

Spencer's stomach twisted. The last thing he, Aldo, and Kate needed right now was a bear army swarming them. How had everything gone so wrong?

"What about the guards?" Evarita chimed in.

Kirby didn't answer right away. Spencer guessed she was consulting whatever feeds she'd managed to restore to the surveillance screen. "They're trying to clear an exit, to get themselves out of there, too. The big guy—Ivan—is moving one of the boulders now! What should I do?!"

"Just keep watching!" Spencer called, bracing himself as Aldo rose up onto his hind legs for a third attack. They were at the head of the path that led into the center of Bearhaven. Once Pam drove in, they'd have buildings on four sides of them. There were pathways out, but Spencer

hoped they were too strewn with debris from the fire for the damaged truck to get through, and Spencer knew Pam would be too afraid, and too proud, to run for it on foot.

The pickup truck spouted a big puff of black smoke and jerked forward.

"He's going in!" Kate cheered as they chased the pickup truck into the center of Bearhaven. Pam steered toward one of the paths at the far side of the clearing.

"I'm going to cut him off!" Aldo called, but just as he started to race forward, another cloud of black smoke coughed out of the pickup truck with a loud bang.

"Aldo, Kate, stay back!" Spencer cried, afraid the truck might suddenly burst into flames. Pam's truck gave another metallic bang and let out an even bigger cloud of black smoke, then screeched to a stop in front of the flagpole. The engine rattled loudly before falling silent. There was one more bang, but Spencer couldn't make anything out through all the pitch-black smoke.

Pam coughed, and Aldo and Kate shuffled back a few steps. *Is Pam out of the truck?* Spencer squinted through the smoke that was just starting to clear.

"I'm guessing the remote is what you're after?" Pam's voice taunted. A second later, Spencer was able to make him out. Pam was standing in the back of the pickup truck now. "*This* remote?" he waved the master remote in the air with one hand. His other hand was tucked behind his back. Spencer gulped. Why was Pam suddenly so confident?

"The bears are out! And so are the guards!" Kirby reported.

Spencer didn't have time to reply. Aldo lunged toward Pam.

"Not so fast!" Pam cried, then pulled a blowtorch out from behind his back and aimed it straight at Aldo.

"Ahh!" Spencer yelled as Aldo skidded to a halt and scrambled back a few steps.

Spencer looked into the bed of the pickup truck. The silver box he'd seen the guards pull blowtorches out of before was standing open.

"You're just like your parents, little Plain," Pam jeered. He waved the blowtorch around like a sword. "You think you're so smart. But look at you now. Trapped. In your own precious *Bearhaven*."

"You're the one who's trapped!" Spencer shouted back at Pam.

"Oh, really?" Pam answered with a smirk.

"Spencer." Kirby's voice was in Spencer's ear. *Not now, Kirby!* he thought.

"Because with this little remote here, I've just commanded all my bears to come to me immediately." Pam waved the remote again. Then his voice dropped out of its singsongy lilt and into a slow menacing threat. "And kill anyone they find in their way."

Spencer's mouth went dry. He could feel Aldo shifting beneath him, as though trying to figure out what to do. Kate let out a small whimper. "You're bluffing," Spencer said. He tried to keep his voice from shaking. But even as he said the words, he knew Pam was telling the truth. He could already hear the thundering footsteps of eighty-seven bears charging toward them.

"Am I?" Pam asked.

"Spencer!" Kirby was in his ear again. "Somebody's coming!"

"I know that!" Spencer hissed, panicking. "Aldo . . ." he started, afraid their only hope was to make a break for the Lab. And they may already be too late to do that.

"No, I mean—" Kirby tried again, but Spencer cut her off.

"Please! Not right now!" Spencer shouted. He felt like his head was going to explode. *What are we going to do!*

"It's too late to plead with me, little Plain," Pam said.

Aldo started to turn slowly in a circle, as though trying to determine how they could possibly defend themselves. When he faced Pam again, movement on the hilltop overlooking Bearhaven caught Spencer's eye. Bearhaven's flag snapped in the breeze, hiding the hill from view for just a second. When it went slack again, Spencer gasped. Pam spun around to see what Spencer had.

"What—? Who—?" Pam stammered.

Bears were fanning out along the ridge. Lots of bears.

"Mom!" Spencer heard Kate whisper from behind Aldo.

Bearhaven's captive bears filled the hilltop.

Vroom! A motorcycle peeled around the pack of bears and gunned straight down the hill at top speed. *Uncle Mark!* Spencer thought. But then he saw long blond hair flying out from under the helmet. *Mom?* Two more motorcycles zoomed out from behind the bears and sped down the hill after the first. Spencer knew they must be Dad and Uncle Mark. They'd arrived at last.

Bearhaven's bears started to stream into the valley after Spencer's family. Spencer swallowed hard. *This isn't over yet.*

37

"They're closing in on us!" Kate cried, drawing Spencer's attention back to the bear army that was approaching fast, with orders to kill. His eyes flew to the path between Raymond's Café and Pinky's Rehab Center, where he could just make out the blur of bears charging toward them. He whirled around and saw that same threatening army approaching the path that led between Pinky's and the shop buildings.

"They're coming for you!" Pam trilled, but just before the first of his bears entered the clearing, Bearhaven's bears intercepted them, fighting them back. Spencer saw Fred Crossburger, Bearhaven's aerobics instructor, rise onto his hind legs to go claw to claw with one of Pam's bears. Beside him, Bunny Weaver, Kate and Aldo's mother, was staring down a honey-colored bear from Pam's army, snapping her teeth and driving the bear away from the path. Bearhaven's bears stretched out on either side of Fred and Bunny, creating a wall between Spencer, Aldo, Kate, and Pam, and Pam's attacking bears.

"Not as fast as you hoped!" Spencer answered, and hopped off Aldo's back, gaining confidence. He dropped his mission pack to the ground and crouched beside Aldo. He scooped a rock off the ground and shoved it into his pocket, then started digging into his bag. A plan was taking shape in his mind. He just needed a way to tell it to his teammates without Pam hearing. "Kate, *hruk!*" Spencer growled the bears' word for "come." Kate stepped closer to Spencer.

"What are you doing?" Pam yelled down at Spencer. *The mission pack is making him nervous!* Spencer realized.

"Aldo, make noise," Spencer muttered. Aldo immediately started to huff, staring at Pam. He thumped the ground with his paws, adding even more noise to the sounds of bears brawling at the entrances to the clearing.

"Tell your bear to leave me alone," Pam ordered anxiously, waving his blowtorch around so that Aldo wouldn't forget about the weapon.

Spencer started to quickly whisper to Kate as he slipped the spare roll of medical tape out of his mission pack into his back pocket. "When I distract Pam, hide under the truck. If you see the remote hit the ground," he hurried on, "grab it as fast as you can and get back under the truck."

Kate didn't answer. She just zeroed her focus in on the space beneath Pam's pickup truck.

"Aldo, when I tell you," Spencer whispered as quickly as he could, "make him think you're attacking, but don't get close enough to get burned." Trusting that the bear had heard him, Spencer finally grabbed the last of what he needed from his mission pack—his slingshot—and leaped to his feet. There was no time now to search the ground for more rocks. He'd have to use what he had. He sprinted around to the side of the pickup truck.

"What's that?" Pam laughed, turning to face Spencer. "A toy slingshot? You're not going to stop someone as powerful as I am with a toy, little Plain. Haven't your parents taught you *anything*?"

Out of the corner of his eye, Spencer saw Kate creep up to the truck and crawl underneath it.

"They've taught me a lot of things!" Spencer shouted. "Like how to treat animals with *respect*! And—" Pam burst out laughing, cutting Spencer off.

"Well, that's nice. But it's not going to help you much." Pam waved the remote around. "I'm still the one holding a remote that controls a bear army, aren't I?"

"Not for long!" Spencer shouted, reaching into his pocket. *"Hachuk!"* Spencer cried the bears' command to attack as he grabbed the rock and loaded it into the slingshot.

Aldo huffed and lunged forward, slamming into the back of the truck. Pam screamed and whirled around to face the bear.

"I warned you!" Pam cried, and blasted the blowtorch at Aldo. The flame streamed farther out of the blowtorch than Spencer had ever expected and hit Aldo in the ear.

"No!" Spencer gasped. He hadn't meant for Aldo to get hurt! The bear stumbled back and dropped to all fours.

Pam cheered for himself. He started to turn back to Spencer triumphantly, but just as he did, Spencer aimed the slingshot straight at Pam's hand and launched the rock at his target.

Ping! The rock hit its mark. The remote flew out of Pam's hand and over the side of the truck.

"Ahh!" Pam shrieked.

Spencer didn't stop to celebrate. He reloaded his slingshot with the only thing he had left to throw—his jade bear.

"You're going to regret that!" Pam hollered, and started to turn away.

Now! Spencer launched the jade bear straight at Pam's head. It flew through the air and struck Pam hard in the temple.

"Oww!" Pam howled, and dropped to his knees in the truck bed, clutching the side of his head.

"Aldo! Keep him there!" Spencer shouted, dropping the slingshot to the ground and grabbing the medical tape from his back pocket.

"Ahh!" Pam shrieked again as Aldo lumbered up into the bed of the truck and towered over Pam, popping his jaw and glaring furiously at the cowering man. Spencer scrambled up into the back of the truck just as Pam started to slide backward, trying to escape Aldo.

Aldo lunged closer to Pam, and Pam threw his hands into the air, shielding his face. His eyes were squeezed shut. "Call him off!" Pam cried.

"No way!" Spencer yelled back, and launched himself in between Aldo and Pam. He grabbed one of Pam's hands out of the air and started to wrap the wrist in medical tape.

"What are you—" Pam started, and lashed out at Spencer with his free hand. Spencer ducked just in time, avoiding the blow, and Aldo swiped a paw at Pam. One of his claws grazed Pam's chest, tearing Pam's silky shirt. "Ahhh!" Pam screamed. "Call him off!" he demanded again, but Spencer ignored Pam and instead grabbed Pam's free hand. He worked quickly to tape it to the first. He wound the medical tape around and around until Pam's two hands were encased in a thick white bulb of tape. Pam tried to kick at Spencer, but Aldo firmly laid a paw on Pam's legs and kept them pressed against the metal truck bed. "You're going to regret this, little Plàin," Pam threatened, his voice low and menacing.

"No, I think *you're* going to regret ever coming to Bearhaven, Pam," Spencer answered, and quickly taped Pam's ankles together while Aldo bared his teeth and held Pam's legs in place.

38

Spencer jumped from the back of the pickup truck to the ground. Aldo landed beside him with a thud.

"Get back here right now!" Pam cried, but Spencer didn't look back. Pam's hands and feet were taped. He wasn't going anywhere. For a moment, they were safe.

Honk! Honk! Honk!

Spencer spun around. That moment was over. A pickup truck with Margo at the wheel sped into the clearing, forcing Bearhaven's wall of bears to break apart to avoid being run over. Pam's bear army started to pour into the clearing behind the truck, racing past Bearhaven's splintered defenses. Bearhaven's bears rushed in with them, still fighting to hold them back. But Spencer could tell it was too late. The bear army had gained too much ground.

"Now what?" Kate cried from under the broken-down pickup truck. It would be a matter of seconds before the bear army and Margo and Ivan were upon them.

"Let me go!" Pam yelled. "This is your last chance! If you want *any hope* of surviving let me go NOW!"

Vroom! Vroom! Vroom! Three motorcycles suddenly sped into the clearing. They overtook the bears and headed straight for the pickup truck. Spencer could see his parents' and uncle's faces now. Relief washed over him. He watched as Uncle Mark pulled something out of the front of his jacket and lobbed it into the open window of the pickup truck. Not a second later, the truck's cab filled with smoke, hiding Margo and Ivan from view. The truck swerved dangerously, and then Margo slammed on the brakes. Mom, Dad, and Uncle Mark circled the truck on their motorcycles, but Spencer didn't wait to find out what they did next. Seeing them in operative mode snapped him back into action.

"Kate! The remote!" he called. The cub scrambled out from under the truck, the remote in her mouth. Spencer grabbed it. Before he could even search for the right button to press, the bear army was on them. Aldo lunged in front of a bear who was going after Spencer, and Kate set off running, trying to outpace a bear on her tail. Zoe emerged from the crowd of bears, and she and Aldo worked to fight the army away from Spencer, but the bears kept coming.

I'm trapped! Bearhaven bears were fighting the microchipped bears all around him, but Pam's bears were trained fighters. Spencer knew that any second one would break through.

"Now what, little Plain?" Pam shouted over the fray. Spencer turned his back on Pam's shouts. He had to think!

The flagpole! It was right in front of him, and too smooth and too narrow for the bears to climb! Spencer raced over to it. He shoved the remote into his back pocket and shimmied up the metal pole. Once he was sure he was a safe distance off the ground, Spencer stopped climbing, his legs and arms wrapped tightly around the pole. He looked down, surprised by how high he'd climbed without being afraid. But there was no time to think about fear now. The clearing below was swarming with bears locked in battle. Off to one side, Dad and Uncle Mark were wrestling Ivan to the ground, and Mom was tying Margo up a few feet away.

Spencer grabbed the remote from his back pocket. "Oh no . . ." he whispered. There were tons of buttons on the remote! Some of them were green, some yellow, some blue, and some red, and every button had a little number on it. But none of them said "attack" or "stop" the way Spencer had expected. Spencer had to find the right buttons and push them in the right order, or there was no telling what the bears in the clearing would do! He could feel himself starting to panic, and he tightened his grip on the flagpole.

"Spencer!" Kirby's voice startled Spencer. "Hit every red button, then the green number one!"

"What?!" Spencer exclaimed.

"Hit every red button, then the green number one!" Kirby repeated.

"How do you know?!"

"I have the users' manual!" Kirby hurried to answer. "I took it from the supply truck when I deactivated the tranquilizer darts faster than you! I wanted to know how the technology worked. Just hit the buttons!"

Spencer looked down at the remote. He pressed the red one, two, three, four, and five, then hovered a thumb over the green number one. He took a deep breath, his eyes on the clearing below. "Here goes nothing." He pressed the green one.

The battle that raged in the center of Bearhaven ended immediately. The microchipped bears returned to all fours or shuffled nervously away from their Bearhaven opponents. And Bearhaven's bears did the same, relieved, Spencer was sure, to be finished fighting.

"NOOOO!" Pam's howl rose up over the eerie quiet that had fallen in the clearing.

"We did it!" Spencer cried over Pam as he started to climb back down the flagpole. "Kirby, you're a genius!" As he climbed he saw one brown-and-black bear push his way through the crowd of bears and take off running. It was Aldo, and Spencer knew exactly where he was going.

39

As soon as Spencer returned to the ground, he pushed his way through the sea of bears, breaking into a jog. "Mom!" he called, and the bears started to move aside for him. "Dad!"

"Spencer!" he heard Mom call back. When Spencer had almost made it all the way through the mass of shocked and exhausted bears, he found Mom and Dad. They were running toward him, calling his name.

"Oh, Spencer!" Mom cried, and pulled him into a hug. Dad didn't wait for his own chance to hug Spencer; he just wrapped his arms around Mom and Spencer both. "I can't believe what you just did!" Mom exclaimed, finally letting Spencer go. "I'm so proud of you!"

"And glad you're all right." Dad pulled Spencer into a second hug, but Spencer gently pushed him away.

"We have to go to the Lab," he started to explain urgently. "B.D.'s really badly hurt." He broke into a jog, heading toward the closest motorcycle. "Come on!" he called. Mom and Dad caught up to him, and Mom climbed onto the motorcycle. She held out her helmet to Spencer and motioned for him to get on the bike behind her.

Spencer took the helmet and climbed on, relieved that his parents weren't pressing him for more information right now. Instead, they seemed to click right back into operative mode.

"Shane, find Pinky and meet us at the Lab," Mom said.

"You got it." Dad stopped where he was. "I'll see you two there." He turned back to the crowd of bears and wove his way in, searching for Pinky.

"Spence!" Uncle Mark called, running over. He gave Spencer's shoulder a squeeze when he reached him. "Glad to see you in one piece, kid. You've turned into quite the operative."

"Thanks, Uncle Mark," Spencer shouted over the sound of Mom starting up the motorcycle.

"B.D.'s hurt," Mom explained to Uncle Mark. "We've got to get to the Lab. Can you—"

"I'll stay here and deal with Pam," Uncle Mark said, as though reading Mom's mind.

"Hold on tight, Spencer!" Mom called. Spencer wrapped his arms around her waist. After all the time he'd spent on Aldo's back, evading Pam and his army over the past few days, holding on tight was something Spencer was *very* good at.

Vroom! Mom sped in a wide arc around the bears, then took the path that cut between the meetinghouse and Raymond's Café. Spencer couldn't help but smile. Mom always warned Uncle Mark to be careful while driving Spencer around in his sports cars, and to be sure not to drive too fast. He could hardly believe he was peeling through Bearhaven now, on the back of a motorcycle *Mom* was driving.

Mom came to a smooth stop beside the Lab, and she and Spencer both hopped off the motorcycle. Spencer tugged the helmet from his head and dropped it on the seat of the bike.

"What happened to B.D.?" Mom asked rushing up to the metal wall of the Lab.

"Pam hit him with his pickup truck . . . really hard," Spencer said, trying to force the memory of the impact out of his mind.

"Has Evarita said anything?"

Spencer shook his head, and Mom breathed on the wall, opening an entrance for herself and Spencer. With a stony expression on her face, Mom rushed into the Lab. Spencer hurried after her.

"Dora!" Mom exclaimed right away. The bear was standing in the doorway to Professor Weaver's lab. She looked back and forth between Spencer and Mom, then nodded into the room silently. She turned to lead the way.

Spencer hung back, afraid of what he'd find. He spotted a discarded BEAR-COM beside the doorway and picked it up, anxious to have something to do with his hands now that his jade bear was gone.

"Is Pinky coming?" he heard Evarita ask quietly as soon as Mom had stepped into the Lab.

"Shane's bringing her now," Mom answered, then went to kneel beside B.D., clearing a space for Spencer to see the bear through the open doorway. The massive black bear lay on a wool blanket in the middle of the floor. He was on his side, his legs tucked up against himself in a way that—if not for his size—made him look almost cub-like. Darwin was curled up against him, his head resting on B.D.'s shoulder.

"I keep telling you," B.D. said, his words coming out slowly, as though each one took everything in him to say. "You don't have to whisper." Nothing except for the bear's mouth moved. He took a long, labored breath. "I'm fine."

"We know, B.D.," Aldo answered, his voice only slightly louder than Mom's and Evarita's had been. He was sitting back on his haunches beside John Shirley, who was no longer wearing a BEAR-COM. They were only a foot or two away from B.D. "It's just been a long day."

B.D. closed his eyes and didn't answer. Spencer shoved John Shirley's BEAR-COM into his pocket and went to kneel beside Mom.

"B.D.," he said, "did they tell you? We beat Pam." He kept his eyes on B.D.'s. "Aldo and I captured Pam." Spencer thought he saw B.D. try to smile at that. "And Mom and Dad and Uncle Mark captured Margo and Ivan. We won't have to worry about any of them coming after Bearhaven again," he went on. "And the bear army is free now."

"My family," Darwin murmured.

"Yes, Darwin," B.D. said slowly. "Family." After a long pause, he met Spencer's eyes again. "Well done," he said. He turned his eyes on Aldo. "Well done," he said again.

"B.D.," Dora said quietly, "save your strength."

"For what?" the bear answered. Everyone in the room fell silent.

"For talking to the bear army," Spencer said, jumping in frantically. Why was everyone acting like B.D. was dying? There wasn't even any blood on the blanket. B.D. was going to be fine. He'd said it himself. He was fine. "I think they're going to be confused about what happens next, and our bears will want to hear from you about the battle, and the new Bearhaven, and—" Mom laid a hand on Spencer's arm. He forgot what he was going to say next. He opened his mouth, desperate to think of something to fill the silent room, but Pinky rushed in just then, with Dad close behind her.

"Let's give Pinky some space to work," Mom said gently, standing up. "Spencer, come with me."

Spencer started to protest, but Mom squeezed his shoulder.

"I'll see you in a little bit, B.D.," he said, then leaned closer to catch the bear's eye. "Well done."

40

"Spencer!" Kate cried as soon as Spencer and Mom left B.D.'s side and stepped out into the Lab's hallway. The special metal of the Lab's outer wall was just sealing shut behind Kate, Professor Weaver, and Bunny. "I can't believe we did it! That was so cool! I thought for sure—" Professor Weaver grunted something, gently interrupting Kate. "B.D.'s going to be okay, isn't he?" the cub asked, her voice hopeful.

Spencer didn't know what to say. He glanced at Mom, but she was looking back and forth between Bunny and Professor Weaver, as though trying to communicate something to them with her eyes. Spencer fumbled to get the BEAR-COM from his pocket and offered it to Professor Weaver. John Shirley wouldn't be wearing it anytime soon. Spencer was sure that after having seen a human run down his brother, John Shirley would return to his old ways of avoiding humans at all costs as soon as possible. Discarding the BEAR-COM was just the first step.

Professor Weaver lowered his head toward Spencer. He and Bunny were two of the kindest bears Spencer had ever met, but now they looked weary. Dark blood was matted in Bunny's silver fur. And when Professor Weaver stepped back, once Spencer had fastened the BEAR-COM around his neck, he limped.

"Thank you, Spencer," Professor Weaver said quietly. "For everything. We'll have plenty to celebrate later, I'm sure. But for now," Professor Weaver returned his attention to Mom, "word is spreading that B.D. is hurt."

"Pinky's with him now," Mom said.

Bunny grunted something as she looked beyond Spencer and Mom. Spencer turned around. Pinky, Dad, Evarita, and Aldo were just stepping into the hallway. A lump rose in Spencer's throat immediately. Evarita had tears in her eyes, and Spencer could tell from the look on his dad's face that B.D. wasn't going to be fine. Spencer reached into his pocket only to remember that the jade bear wasn't there.

"How is B.D. doing?" Spencer asked, his voice shaking.

Dad put his hands in his pockets and took a deep breath. "B.D.'s injuries are bad," he said.

"But Pinky's here, she can fix them!" Spencer answered.

Dad shook his head. "He can't move any of his legs, Spencer, and he's having trouble breathing now." Spencer felt Mom wrap an arm around him, and pull him close against her side. He looked to Pinky in confusion.

Pinky started to speak in Ragayo. When she finished, Professor Weaver translated. "She says he's badly hurt on the inside. There's nothing she, or anyone, can do now."

"But he said he was fine!" Spencer protested, twisting away from Mom. "B.D.'s going to be fine."

"I'm sorry, Spencer," Dad said, his voice heavy with

emotion. "B.D. is a strong bear, and a brave bear, but his injuries are too serious." Spencer felt tears start to well in his eyes. It wasn't fair! B.D. had only been protecting his sister—his family!

"We have to let him go," Mom said quietly.

"May we see him?" Professor Weaver asked. The Weavers were huddled together now, Kate had buried her face in Professor Weaver's fur, and Bunny and Aldo were leaning against one another, shoulder to shoulder, as though holding each other up.

"In a minute," Dad answered. "Dora and John Shirley wanted a moment alone with him."

"Excuse me?" Kirby stepped into the hallway tentatively. "I wasn't sure if I should still be watching the surveillance screens, but I thought you should know—" Kirby hesitated.

"What is it?" Professor Weaver asked.

"There are a ton of bears outside," Kirby answered. "They're filling the clearing around the Lab."

Bunny said something quietly in Ragayo, and Pinky nodded solemnly.

"Yes," Professor Weaver answered. "They're waiting for news . . . about B.D."

"He's gone," Dora said. She padded out into the hallway and came to stand beside Mom. Tears started to pour down Spencer's cheeks.

"I'm so sorry, Dora," Mom murmured.

Dora nodded. "He fought for his family—" She hesitated, collecting herself. "And for Bearhaven until the very end."

"He was one of the bravest bears we have ever known," Professor Weaver said. "I'll tell the others."

"In a moment," Dora said as Darwin's cries carried out of the room behind them. He and John Shirley appeared in the door. "Let's just take a moment."

Mom reached out a hand and gently stroked Dora's shoulder, then pulled Spencer into a hug. Dad stepped closer, wrapping his arms around the two of them.

41

One Week Later

"Ouch, Zoe!" Aldo ducked his head away from Zoe, who was replacing the bandage on his burned ear.

"I thought the Head of the Bear Guard was supposed to be brave," Zoe muttered, shooting Spencer a look. Spencer laughed, nearly choking on his slice of peanut butter toast. He set it down on the Weavers' brand-new kitchen table and reached for his glass of water.

"I thought medical problems were taken care of by Pinky!" Aldo answered playfully, moving his head back into Zoe's reach. Spencer knew the honor of being named the next Head of the Bear Guard still hadn't worn off for Aldo. And today marked the bear's first day on the job in the new Bearhaven. Spencer didn't think there was much that could get Aldo down.

"My mom's training me, remember?" Zoe answered. "She says I'm going to be as good at this stuff as she is one day."

Zoe picked up where she'd left off with Aldo's ear, making Aldo flinch.

"Well, obviously that day isn't today!" Aldo teased.

Spencer started to laugh again.

"What's so funny?" Kate asked, bounding into the room. Her chestnut-colored fur was still dulled by the last of the soot from her Darwin disguise. She claimed it wouldn't come out in all the river swims she'd taken in the few days since everyone had arrived in the new Bearhaven, but Spencer thought she was keeping her fur a little dirty for a reason—she didn't want anyone to forget the role she'd played in defeating Pam.

Before Spencer could answer the cub, Dad poked his head through the front door.

"Are you all ready?" he asked.

"Almost," Zoe answered for herself and Aldo.

"Same here," Spencer chimed in, then picked up the tablet from the kitchen table and started to dial a video call.

"You're calling now?" Kate asked, hurrying over to Spencer's side. She jutted her head right up next to his so that the camera would capture her face, too, when the call connected.

"Hi, Spencer! Hi, Kate!" Kirby said as soon as her face appeared on the screen. "How's the new Bearhaven? Is it as cool as the original one?"

"Hi, Kirby!" Kate cried happily.

"Hi, Kirby," Spencer said. "We're about to leave for the ceremony. You can see the new Bearhaven on the way there."

Spencer picked his backpack up off the floor beside his seat and tucked the tablet into a little pocket he'd made for it. He was sure to leave the tablet's camera and some of the screen sticking out over the top of the pocket so that Kirby would be able to see. Today's ceremony was to celebrate Bearhaven's victory over Pam, and the free bears, Spencer, and Kirby were going to be honored for their bravery. Bearhaven's flag would be raised, marking the new Bearhaven as the official home of the bears, and B.D.'s flag would go up, to memorialize his bravery. Kirby deserved to be there as much as anyone. Spencer stood up and swung the bag onto his back.

"Okay, it's done!" Zoe said triumphantly, stepping back from Aldo to admire the ear she'd bandaged.

"Thanks, Zoe," Aldo said, heading for the door. "Come on, we shouldn't be late." Spencer and Zoe followed Aldo out of the Weavers' new house, and Kate trotted along behind so that she could stay in the camera's view.

Mom, Dad, Dora, and Darwin were waiting on the front path.

"Hi, Spencer," Darwin said as soon as Spencer stepped out into the morning sun. Ever since B.D.'s death and John Shirley's return to the wild, Darwin had gotten even more attached to Dora's side. Now Spencer rarely saw the cub without his mother.

"Look who's here, Darwin," Spencer said, then turned around so that the tablet would face the cub.

"Kirby!" Darwin exclaimed happily.

"Hi, Darwin!" she said.

"She's coming to the ceremony with us," Spencer said, turning back around. "But we'd better go before we miss it!"

Dad slung an arm around Spencer's shoulders. "Something tells me they wouldn't start without you," he said as they all began to walk. Spencer smiled. He could hear Kate chattering to Kirby behind him, pointing out the new Bearhaven's landmarks as they passed them, and the areas that had been marked for the new Pinky's Rehab Center, and the new Lab.

They took a path that led through trees and newly built bear homes until they reached a small field that was surrounded on three sides by a rushing river. An empty flagpole stood in the center of the field.

"Looks like most of the bears are already here," Mom said, sliding her sunglasses up into her blond hair as she looked into the field where almost two hundred bears were gathered. The bracelet with the gold bear charm slipped down her wrist and glittered in the sunshine. Spencer slipped a hand into his pocket. The jade bear was there—Spencer had recovered it after the battle against Pam's army.

Mom gave Spencer's shoulder a squeeze. "We'll see you after, Spencer," she said, then added for the millionth time, "We couldn't be more proud."

"Good luck," Dad said before following Mom into the crowd of bears.

"Thanks!" Spencer called. He hurried to catch up with Aldo, Zoe, Dora, Darwin, and Kate. They made a wide loop around the crowd, then cut in to the flagpole, where a space was cleared. Ro Ro, Kenny, Raymond, and Marguerite were waiting for them there. Spencer took his place beside the group he couldn't help but still think of as the free bears.

"Here," he said to Kate, who was sitting next to him. "Will you take Kirby?" He slipped the backpack off his back and propped it up against one of Kate's front legs so that Kirby was facing out into the audience of Bearhaven's bears.

Kate bowed her head over the tablet, checking on Kirby, then looked out at the crowd herself, obviously pleased to be Kirby's perch.

Spencer spotted Mom and Dad as they joined Uncle Mark and Evarita in the crowd, then he caught Professor Weaver's eye. The bear was standing in the front row. He nodded at Spencer, giving him the signal.

Spencer walked over to the trunk that stood at the bottom of the flagpole and opened it. Bearhaven's two flags lay folded inside. Spencer took a deep breath and pushed the black-and-silver Bearhaven flag aside, reaching instead for the scrap of green-and-gold fabric that had, until today, been known as Dora's flag. It was a scrap of one of the jerseys she, B.D., and John Shirley had been made to wear as mascots for Gutler University before they were rescued.

A lump rose in Spencer's throat. B.D. had been the one to tell him about Dora's flag. They flew it to remember what the bears of Bearhaven had sacrificed and what they'd gained, B.D. had said. It would fly over the new Bearhaven for the same reasons now, but also to remember B.D. To always remember B.D. With shaking hands, Spencer reached for the rope attached to the flagpole. A hush went over the field, leaving Spencer to raise B.D.'s flag in silence.

After watching the flag shimmer in the sunlight at the top of the flagpole for a long, quiet moment, Spencer returned to the trunk. He pulled the second flag out, its silver crown flashing, and reached again for the flagpole.

Freedom for all bears, Spencer thought, watching Bearhaven's flag rise over the field. Behind him, he knew almost two hundred free bears were watching the flag and thinking the same thing. It had been a close fight, but this flag flying over the new Bearhaven today meant that Spencer and the bears had won. They'd defeated Pam, once and for all.

Once the flag was raised, Spencer returned to his spot beside Kate. Aldo stepped out of the line of free bears. He looked out over the crowd of bears in the field, and a chorus of grunts and cheers rose from the crowd.

"Welcome," Aldo said, his voice louder, and stronger, than Spencer had ever heard it. "Welcome home."

Property of SPENCER PLAIN

Notes for the Evacuation

● Sleuth #1: In the wild, "sleuth" means a group of bears. In the evacuation, it's a group that's supposed to stick together and is assigned to the same checkpoint.

B.D. (Head of the Guard and the sleuth!)

Aldo

Kate

Darwin

John Shirley

Me

● Remember which tree is the sleuth #1 checkpoint and go there every night.

● In an emergency, get as close to the sleuth #1 checkpoint as I can, then hide in a tree. Mark the trunk with a rough X that looks like natural bear markings so that Bearhaven bears can find me.

• Stash enough food for four days in the forest before getting relocated:

Peanut butter sandwiches

Raymond's fuel bars

Apples

Bearhaven's flag

= Freedom for all bears. Kate says the crown on the bear claw is a symbol of bears being their own masters.

Ragayo Words:

Galuk = hurry   Abragan = for the bears

Hruk = come   Grauk = go

Ko = now   Hachuk = attack

Shala = safe   Anbranda = friend

Learn more about the bears of Bearhaven, and continue the adventure with Spencer and Kate at www.secretsofbearhaven.com.

EGG IN THE HOLE PRODUCTIONS THANKS:

Erin Black, for her continued dedication to the world of Bearhaven, and Nancy Mercado, David Levithan, and Ellie Berger for their support.

Ross Dearsley for capturing the characters of Bearhaven so completely through illustration and Nina Goffi for her beautiful book design.

The marketing and publicity team at Scholastic, for always finding new ways to share Bearhaven with readers: Antonio Gonzalez, Rachel Feld, Jazan Higgins, and Lori Benton.

Paul Gagne, Executive Producer, Paul Ruben, Director, and Louisa Gummer, Narrator, for their creative talent in bringing Bearhaven to audio.

For their enthusiastic and ongoing expert advice and contributions to the world of Bearhaven: Dr. Thomas Spady, Bear Biologist, California State University San Marcos, and Dr. Sherri Wells-Jensen, Linguist, Bowling Green State University.

Emma D. Dryden and Elizabeth Grojean, for enthusiastic editorial and managerial creativity and support.

Finally, thank you to all the administrators, teachers, librarians, and students who have welcomed Bearhaven into their schools!

ABOUT THE AUTHOR

K. E. Rocha is the author of the Secrets of Bearhaven, developed in collaboration with Egg in the Hole Productions. She received a BA in English from Trinity College and an MFA from New York University. She has never visited with talking bears, although she often talks to her goofy little hound dog, Reggie, while writing in her apartment in Brooklyn, New York.